P9-CRG-959
THE
BOOK

ERIC KAHN GALE

An Imprint of HarperCollins*Publishers*

To Whom It May Concern:

You must have gone through a lot to get this book in your hands, and I'm not sure what you think you're about to read.

But whatever it is, you're wrong.

This is a record of The Bully Book and what it did to me.

How I fought it, and the way it fought back.

Once, I thought The Bully Book was a myth.

Then maybe a mystery I could solve.

Now I know it's a monster and I'm trying to defeat it.

Are you with me . . .

or The Book?

How to Make Trouble without Getting in Trouble, Rule the School, and Be the Man

That title is too long, but it gets the job done. The main message of this manual is:

Get the job done.

I'm in sixth grade. I've been stuck in school since kindergarten and I've learned a few things.

I'm an observer. I see what works and what doesn't.

Why does a joke sound funny coming from one kid but seem stupid when someone else says it? Why do some kids have to eat alone while others are rolling in friends? These are the questions I've been thinking about.

I'm here to tell you—I've got the answers.

This year, I survived the school district merger, outsmarted kids ten times my size, and completely conquered sixth grade. I've got a ton of friends, everybody does what I say, and teachers don't mess with me. This has been the best year of my life and I made it all by myself.

How'd I do it? That's what I'm about to tell you.

Journal #1

For as long as I can remember, all I wanted was to be normal and stay out of trouble. And I've done that pretty well for the last 11 years. But today was the first day of 6th grade, and things got a little strange.

When I came into the classroom, Jason Crazinsky already had Melody Miller by the shoulders and was telling her to stand still. I'm getting mad just thinking about it. I hate the way he was touching her.

It was a few minutes before first period and everyone crowded around Jason and Melody. He raised his left foot in the air and looked at her intensely. She shivered.

This was a "karate demonstration," and Jason has done this kind of thing to kids before. I keep a low enough profile so I never get chosen for this stuff, but I didn't like that he was picking on Melody. Me and her go all the way back to kindergarten. When we used to play House she'd always be my mom, so now that we're older I feel pretty protective. I got ready to charge Jason, counter his karate moves, and break her out of his grip.

"Kah-hah-yah!" He kicked his foot three times, inches away from her nose, then stepped back and bowed for the class before I could even make a move. Melody stood there frozen.

"That's amazing," someone said. Jason just smiled. He's a skinny kid, but strong. His face makes him look like he's angry all the time. Though maybe he just is. Jason always wants to challenge you to an arm-punching contest. Or to show you his black belt. "Kung fu!" yelled Adrian Noble. "You could demolish somebody with that."

"Ka-ra-te," Jason corrected him. "And it is used only in self-defense."

Yeah, like defending yourself against a tiny girl you've pinned against the wall. That's why I call him Jason Crazypants.

"Thanks for saving me, Eric." Melody walked over and pushed me with her palm. "Were you just standing there the whole time?"

"Sorry!" I said. "What could I do? I don't wanna mess with Crazypants."

"You're a lame-o, and he's a butt-hole." Melody started shouting to no one in particular. "Everybody in this grade needs to grow up!"

I think Melody is as loud as she is because she's short. People would look right over her head if she weren't yelling down there.

"We're not little kids anymore," she went on. "When will you get that through your thick heads, people?"

"Hey hey hey . . . " I whispered, ushering her across the room.

It's too early to be starting trouble. I just want things to go smoothly this year.

In our small-town district, 6th grade is the last year of elementary school. Everybody feels too old to still be here, and I think it's making people act weird. We're the biggest kids in the school now, so I guess we've got nobody to worry about except ourselves.

Mr. Whitner walked into the classroom and tried to get our attention, but everyone was busy saying hi to friends they hadn't seen all summer. I looked around the room for Donovan.

Whitner told us that the seats we picked today would be permanent. I think the classroom exploded.

The words had barely left his mouth and butts were

slamming into chairs. The people we sat next to today would seal our fates for the year. Melody grabbed me by the chin and whipped my face around.

"Hey, come on!" she yelled, and yanked me into a seat next to hers. Melody doesn't ask for your opinion, but I was glad she wanted to sit next to me.

There was an empty seat to the left of me and I put my hand on it. A second later, I yelped when Colin Greene sat down on my fingers. He's the biggest loser in my grade, six years running. Through his worn-out sweatpants, I felt a moistness I'd rather leave a mystery.

"S-sorry," Colin spit at me, getting up.

I pulled back my hand, wiping spittle off the side of my face.

"I'm saving this seat for Donovan," I said.

My best friend, Donovan White. Ever since we were partners for a social studies project in 4th grade and we reenacted the entire Civil War. I stayed up all night, reading Wikipedia and writing the script while Donovan made a heavy-metal playlist to go along with the action. We acted all the parts ourselves. I was better at the generals and he played a very convincing corpse.

"Where is Donovan?" I said to Melody.

A smile stretched across her face. "Working on sausage number four."

Donovan's fat, and Melody can be kind of a turd. But I like that about them.

The door to the classroom opened, and somebody came through it, but it wasn't Donovan. Not the guy I knew.

The long, limp blond hair was gone, hair that people always told him would look nice if he were a girl. It was buzzed short, like he was an army guy. The braces had disappeared. Big horse teeth hung out of his mouth because his upper lip was too short to cover them. And something else was missing too, about 25 pounds of boob, butt, and stomach.

"Donovan!" I yelled. "I saved you a seat, man. What happened to you?"

I knew he'd been away at camp the whole summer, but this was ridiculous.

He walked right past me.

"Big D!" called Adrian Noble, the class giant. "Over here, man!" Adrian wears prescription sports goggles instead of glasses. Just in case he needs to tackle you on the way to the water fountain.

"Donovan, hey," I yelled again. "I saved you a seat."

"Grunt!" Jason Crazypants stood up. His perma-angry face glared at me. "Shut your dumb mouth," he said.

The classroom was still noisy, so Mr. Whitner didn't notice.

"What did he say?" I asked Melody.

"Don't listen to him," she said, loud enough for Jason to hear. "He's a jerk."

I turned back to them, but now Donovan was the one standing up. He was staring at me too, like I was a total stranger. And he didn't have nearly enough lip to cover his scowl.

*****

Melody and me stayed away from Donovan the rest of the day, but when her mom picked her up outside of school, I didn't know what to do. Donovan and I always rode the bus together.

But he and Jason Crazypants both got a ride with Adrian Noble's dad. They were pushing each other and laughing.

I rode the bus alone today, for maybe the first time ever.

Paperwork

Let me tell you about something called the Social Order. You can't see it, smell it, or touch it, but it's everywhere and it controls everything. It says who's cool, who's lame, and who's not worth talking to.

What is it saying about you? Look around your class. Where do you fit in?

If you're at the top, you can probably stop reading this book right now. But if you're not, and 99 percent of people aren't, then the Social Order probably isn't too fun. It tells people that it's okay to make fun of you, and laugh at you, and treat you like crap. It probably feels like there's no good reason, and it's totally random, and you've got no control.

But what if I told you that you do have control? That there's a way to change your position, your popularity, and how people treat you?

Draw up a chart. Let's call it a Class Coolness Chart. At the top, write the name of the most popular kid in your class and then every other kid in order until you get to the least popular kid.

But here's the catch: Don't write how it is in your class. Write how you want it to be.

Take some time to do this now.

If you set things up the right way, the Social Order of your class will eventually look like your chart. That's what this book is about.

The two most important positions are the names at the top and the bottom. The name at the top should be you.

If your name isn't at the top, just throw this manual away right now—you don't have the heart to do what comes next.

Still with me?

Good, 'cause now you're gonna realize the second most important name is the one at the bottom. The Grunt. I'll tell you how to pick him out later, because it's very specific.

The Grunt is the key to the entire plan.

Journal #2

We had music class today, which in 5th grade meant singing "In the Jungle" in unison, but this year, we were getting real instruments.

"What are you gonna pick?" Melody said to me as we walked down the hall.

"A trumpet," I said. I blew into my hands and made a trumpeting noise.

"Yeah," she said. "Hopefully the real thing will sound less fartlike."

"Depends on which end I play it from," I said.

"Eww!" Melody laughed and pushed me against the wall.

"Let's keep it moving up there," Mr. Whitner said. He always seems stressed out about something.

In music class, I wanted to sit next to Melody, but the teacher had already made a seating chart and put it up on the board. When I got to my assigned seat, I found Adrian Noble, Jason Crazypants, and Donovan White surrounding me on all sides. They weren't sitting where they were supposed to, but I guess Music Lady didn't notice.

When it came time to get our instruments, I looked at Melody across the room. She made a fart noise with her hands. I smiled and turned to Donovan.

"What instrument are you gonna pick?" I whispered.

He didn't turn his head. I asked him again and his eyes widened.

Music Lady opened a box about the size of a desk drawer.

"Okay, everyone. Let's pass these out!"

She grabbed a white plastic pipe with holes in it and held it in the air.

"A recorder!" she said. "It's like a clarinet, but made of plastic, so it's cheap enough that everyone can have one!"

I set mine down on a music stand. Melody caught my eye from across the room. She shook her head and pretended to stab herself in the eye with the recorder. I wished I had just broken the rules like Jason and them and sat with Melody.

Music Lady told us to try making a sound. I reached for my recorder, but it wasn't on the stand. I looked to see if it had dropped on the floor. I popped my head under my chair.

A horrible sound straightened me up. Thirty terrible musicians blowing spit and bad breath into thirty awful instruments. I put my hands on my lap.

"Excuse me, young man," Music Lady said over the crowd. "Where is your recorder?"

"Uh . . ." I looked around again. Jason Crazypants was sitting at my right.

"I don't know."

"You just received it a minute ago. What is your name?"

"Eric Haskins." The class quieted and turned its attention to me. The silence was worse than the playing.

"Well, Mr. Haskins," Music Lady said, louder than she needed to. "That recorder is school property. You'll do well to find it."

"Yes, ma'am," I said, and I got out of my chair. Kids around me started giggling. Everyone looked.

"We can wait," said Music Lady.

I picked up my backpack and emptied it. I got down on the floor and crawled under my chair. I said excuse me to Jason Crazypants and checked under his chair. He put his hand over his crotch and said, "Don't look at my nuts, man." A few kids laughed.

"I wasn't . . ." Sweat formed above my eyebrows. This was taking too long. On my hands and knees, I crawled over to where Adrian Noble sat.

"Ugh, get away from me, gaywad!" He pushed me to the floor and some guys behind me laughed. I guess Music Lady didn't see.

"We're still waiting," she said. I turned to Donovan, who had been sitting to my left.

He was staring down at his lap. Guilty-like.

"I think you guys took it," I said, standing up.

"What'd you say?" Jason Crazypants grabbed hold of my sleeve.

"You guys took my recorder." I pulled away from him. "One of you three."

"Boys," Music Lady said. "Did you take Mr. Haskins's instrument?"

"They did," I said. The three of them traded a look. "They're not even sitting in their assigned seats."

Jason could barely contain his glee. "You're tripping, Haskins," he said with a laugh. "Your recorder is right there."

He pointed at my music stand, and a white plastic tube sat there, rocking gently, like it'd just been set down.

"Oh!" Music Lady laughed at me. "Too quick to blame,

Mr. Haskins. Now back to our instruments!"

The recorders squealed and I sat down. Melody mouthed, "It's okay," from across the room.

I tried to blow into my recorder, but I didn't have much breath. Jason Crazypants whispered in my ear.

"You gonna cry, Haskins?"

I wasn't, but my throat swelled up when he said it. I hate how that happens.

"You're a loser," Adrian Noble muttered from behind me. Donovan sat silent.

"I am not," I said back.

"You can't help it," Jason said. "It comes with being unpopular."

He smiled. "It comes with being the Grunt."

What Is the Grunt?

The Grunt is a person. But it is also something that you create.

By the time you're done, the Grunt will be the loser of all losers to everyone in your class.

Your job is to make that happen, and the best way to do it is to make fun of the Grunt in front of everybody.

Call the Grunt names, make fun of how the Grunt looks or acts or talks. And make sure everybody can see and hear so they all get the idea.

Eventually, the class will catch on, and they'll start working on the Grunt for you. But in the beginning, you'll have to do all the work. This is a good thing because putting the Grunt on the bottom is a nice way to show you're on the top.

And it can be pretty fun.

Journal #3

For some insurance/lawsuit/nonexistent reason, we still take group bathroom breaks . . . in 6th grade.

The whole class lines up against the wall, and we go in four at a time. Today, The Evil Three stood next to me so we would be in a bathroom group together.

Now my usual way to do my private business involves puffing out my elbows and locking my eyes on the wall in front of me.

I guess this isn't everyone's method.

Adrian Noble grabbed my arm and peeked his head over my shoulder, looking at me pee.

"Toxic!" he screamed.

Jason Crazypants grabbed my other arm.

"Sick!" he yelled. "This gaywad's toxic!"

I've never claimed to pee flowers, but this was definitely an unfair situation. I pulled my arms free and tried to cover myself. I needed to get out of there. I had to pee faster.

I cursed my mother for packing me 2 Hi-Cs. I was tied to the urinal by a liquid rope.

Mr. Whitner called, "What's going on in there?" Everyone could hear what was going on.

"It's Eric Haskins!" Crazypants screamed. "He peed on himself!"

Outside the bathroom, there was silence. Maybe they don't believe him, I thought. Jason Crazypants is a liar—everybody knows that.

I was almost finished. I could run out and tell them it's not true. He tried to watch me pee. I could turn it all around on him.

When I zipped up, I felt the truth. I'd panicked when they tried to look at me.

My pants were darkened with something . . . and it wasn't Hi-C.

Mr. Whitner entered the bathroom and immediately took charge. He ordered The Evil Three out and told Jason Crazypants to lead the kids back to the classroom. I could only imagine what he was going to tell them. Melody wouldn't believe a thing. But Donovan followed him out like a dog.

"Here," Mr. Whitner said, holding a ream of brown paper towel. "Pat yourself dry."

Mr. Whitner's never struck me as someone especially in control. But even with his bad comb-over and thin white dress shirt, he seemed almost heroically in charge.

I patted my pants until you couldn't even see the wet spot, but I still felt dirty.

"Sorry you've gotta see this," I sighed to Whitner.

"Don't worry about it," he said.

"No, seriously," I told him. "I'm not usually like this."

"Bad things can happen to anybody, Eric," he said. "Trust me."

We tossed the dirty paper towel and Whitner asked if I wanted to be sent home for the day.

"Like you wouldn't believe."

He told me he didn't have the authority to excuse someone. Only Principal Clark could do that.

"It's one of the New Rules," he said.

Clark got promoted from assistant principal this year, and he's trying to change everything at school. He held a big assembly where he laid out all of these New Rules.

He says they're to make the school better, but it really just means there's a lot of new ways to get in trouble.

The principal's office is at the end of the New Side of

the school. So I had to walk through the Old Side corridor in pee-smelling pants.

When we got inside his office, Clark was filling out some paperwork. He looked up at us, looked down, and then swept his arm across the entire desk, knocking all his papers to the floor.

"I'm dropping everything . . . literally!" he howled. "What's going on?"

Principal Clark's office is like an altar to himself. It's a time capsule of his life on earth. If an apocalypse happened and the only thing left was this office, at least aliens would know that Principal Tony Clark was once 11th-grade MVP of the basketball team.

Mr. Whitner faked a laugh and I looked at all the crap Clark had just knocked onto the carpet. I guessed his secretary would be the one to clean it up.

"Hello, Mr. Clark," Whitner mumbled. "You know Eric Haskins."

"I never forget a face. Like an elephant that way." Clark shook my hand and winked at me. "Except the only trunk I've got is in the back of my car."

I was secretly glad I hadn't washed.

Mr. Whitner explained to Clark that I'd had an accident in the bathroom.

"Well, it's better to have aimed and missed than never to have aimed at all," Clark interrupted.

Whitner forced a smile and I felt my face heat up. I'm not some idiot who can't use the bathroom. Though I doubt a guy like Clark could understand my predicament.

He only got serious when Whitner said they should let me go home for the day.

He put his fingers to his lips and frowned at me. I thought he'd tell me I had cancer.

"No change of clothes?"

"Sorry, sir," I said.

"This should be one of the New Rules: Be Prepared for Anything," Clark said. "Hard to enforce, though . . ."

I looked at Whitner for help.

"Sometimes the best thing is to just try it again tomorrow," he said. "Why not let Eric phone his mother? I need to get back to class."

How this chimp got to be principal while a stand-up guy like Whitner's stuck wrangling 6th graders is a mystery to me. If I had to guess, I'd say it's because Clark has better hair. It's more principal-y. We're not living in a fair world.

Clark was silent for a minute, and I thought it was because Whitner's logic had shut him up. But it was actually because Clark was thinking. Which I've learned can be a very dangerous thing.

"Eric." Clark smiled. "What about your gym class?"

Oh no, I thought.

"This is one of my favorite New Rules: All 6th graders must keep gym clothes at school. Now that probably seemed like a hassle when you first heard about it. But now it's covering your butt, literally." Clark burst out laughing and buzzed his secretary to clean the mess from the floor.

*****

I didn't need to wonder what Jason Crazypants had told all the kids in class. I didn't need to wonder what they were saying about me.

When I came back wearing bright yellow running shorts, I heard all about it.

The Inner Circle

If you follow the plan in this book carefully, everyone will be your friend, but you need to start somewhere.

You need to pick lieutenants, loyal friends who can help you carry out my instructions. You should have at least two. Your right and left arm.

You'll be spending a lot of time with these kids, so pick them out carefully.

See, people don't think about it much, but the friends you choose can make you miserable.

Friends usually do the same stuff, so you end up in competition with them. The closer you are to your friends, the more it hurts when you fight. If they want to, your friends can really ruin your life.

So find people who can help you but won't be a threat. Avoid kids who might get jealous and want to be on top themselves.

Pick kids who are dumber than you so they'll listen to you.

Pick kids who are stronger than you so they'll protect you.

Pick kids who are followers so that you can lead them to greatness.

Tell them the secrets you learn in this book, but only what they need to know. You are its keeper.

Journal #4

I was like a wounded animal. Laying low. Hiding myself in the long grasses of the savannah.

The Bathroom Disaster was not behind me. I wanted answers. Donovan sat in the back of the bus this afternoon, all by himself. I don't know where Jason and Adrian were.

I sat in the front, staying as far away from him as I could. I skipped my stop. I didn't plan on getting home on time. We rode the bus for another two miles, until it creaked to a stop at the long dirt driveway to Donovan's house. I slunk back in my seat as he walked up the aisle. He didn't see me.

I tailed him for a good quarter of a mile. His walk was noisy, awkward.

We hit the tree line in the foresty part of the neighborhood. Donovan's house is guarded by two enormous trees, and that's where I called him out.

"You're a real traitor, you know," I said, my voice shaking. Donovan froze midstep. His shoulders tensed and finally he turned to face me.

"Why'd you follow me?" he said.

"'Cause you've been following me!" I yelled back. "With your new friends, torturing me."

"Listen," he said, "it's not how I wanted—"

"We were friends, Donovan," I said. "Now you won't even talk to me."

"I am talking to you."

"Out here you are, when no one's watching. Why are you doing this to me?"

"It's not me, Eric," he said. "I swear. It's The Book."

"It is you, Donovan. You're the one doing it."

"It's The Book!" His face reddened. "It's the one that chose you, not me. We've got no choice who's the Grunt!"

"I don't understand what you're saying."

"You're the only one that fit the description. I told them not to choose you, but you're the only one that fits the Grunt. It's in The Book!"

"Wait," I said. "Just shut up for a minute."

Donovan was looking at me wildly. He gripped the straps of his backpack.

"What book?" I said to him. "Why do you guys keep

calling me Grunt?"

Donovan leaned against one of the two mammoth trees. His skin was red and blotchy. He buried his face in his hand and yelled into his palm.

"Get out of here!" His words bounced around the trees. "You can't talk to me now. You'll ruin it. Go!"

His whole body quaked as he shouted. I could see there was still a little man boob left.

Knowing when I'm not wanted, I took the long way home.

In the Family

This book isn't something you can just read alone in your room. You're going to talk to your lieutenants about it. You're going to have meetings about it. But you're not going to be stupid about it.

Don't meet where people can hear you.

Don't brag about it to your cousin.

And don't leave this book around where anybody can find it.

Information like this is worth more when fewer people know about it.

It's like the lottery. If you knew what the winning lottery numbers were going to be, that information would be worth a million dollars. But if ten million people knew what the winning lottery numbers were going to be, they'd all buy tickets and split up the prize. That information would be worth ten cents.

So keep your mouth shut.

Keep other people's mouths shut.

Journal #5

Mr. Whitner gave us a take-home assignment with partners, which can be pretty miserable if you pair up with the wrong kid. I was planning on asking Melody, but Jason Crazypants got to her first.

She hates him just as much as I do, but still said she'd be his partner. That doesn't make any sense to me, unless she's gonna try and sabotage his grade.

Regardless, I can't find another partner. Everyone paired up too quick. Or maybe it's that nobody wants to have anything to do with me. The only other guy without a partner is Colin Greene.

So, it's come to this.

Colin's house is a little like Colin himself. It's small, messy, and a teensy bit sweaty. Colin wore a blue sweatpant/shirt combination like usual and he led me through the house. Colin's hair is a wild mess and his lips shine with spit that leaps out at you with every consonant he speaks, even l's and m's.

"Before we start on the assignment," Colin sputtered, "we can play video games."

Colin led me down a winding hall to his room. I stepped around stains in the carpet and experienced that paranoid feeling I get in summer when mosquitoes are all over me. Stuff kept touching me, or at least that's what it felt like. I was jumpy.

Black painted silhouettes were framed and hanging up on the walls. Two paper shadows shaped like boys. I ended up in front of a doorway and I realized I'd stopped moving. Another shadow crowded in a corner, not like the pictures on the wall. It was a dark shape, messy hair and an enormous figure. My eyes adjusted to the dark and I could see it looking at me. It smiled. I ran down the hall toward Colin.

In his room sat an outdated television, worse than the one in my basement. Colin had an old Wii, the same system as me.

"We can play Wii wallyball," said Colin. "I just need to start the timer."

"What timer?" I said. Colin grabbed a white clock from behind the television.

"I need to start the TV timer," he said. "I only get one hour of screen time a day, so I've gotta use this timer to clock myself."

I picked up my jaw from the floor. "That's not okay," I said. "How can they do that to you?"

"My parents say TV is bad for the eyes," Colin said. He adjusted his thick, eyeball-magnifying glasses. My vision is 20/20 and I watch TV constantly.

"I watched a cartoon show during breakfast"—Colin's shiny lips puckered and stretched as he spoke—"that took up half my hour today, and I was on the computer for 16 minutes—that counts, too. So that means . . ."

"We have 14 minutes to play a game," I answered.

The afternoon was more eventful than I'd expected.

After our extreme gaming session, I still didn't feel like doing the assignment, so Colin and I sat reading his comics collection. I watched the way he slobbered on his fingers before turning each page, so I used a tissue from the bathroom to flip through a detective comic.

When the door swung open, Colin's face broke into panic.

"Ever learn to knock?" he shouted. A monster lumbered into the room. His glossy red lips curled up in a sneer. His greasy brown hair dangled in front of dark little eyes. An oversize T-shirt, its days of clean whiteness long gone, was sweaty and stuck to his skin. This was the shadow monster I had passed by in the hallway. This was Colin's 7th-grade brother. This was Richard.

"What are you two losers doing?" He laughed.

"Reading comics," I answered.

"Oh," he mumbled, looking confused. "Well, that's dumb." He sat down on Colin's bed.

His butt sank the mattress and Colin heated with rage.

"If it's so dumb, Richard, then-why-don't-you-get-out-of-my-room!"

"You get out of your room," said Richard.

"It's mine!" Colin screeched. He rolled onto his back and thrust his bare heels at his brother. Richard coughed and reared up on the bed. His entire weight dropped on Colin's fragile body, crushing him. Colin's fingers caught Richard's hair and yanked as his brother mushed his palm against Colin's nose.

"Hey!" I shouted. "Cut it out, you idiots!"

They froze. Colin let go of the hair and Richard slowly rolled off him.

"And who do you think you are?" said Richard.

"Well, I think my name is Eric," I told him. "Eric Haskins."

Richard looked me up and down.

"Eric Haskins. You're in Colin's grade." His red face pulsed as he spoke. "Lemme ask you, how big of a loser is my brother?"

"Not as big a loser as you," I said. I meant it in every possible way. Richard was large.

"Hey, don't you call me that!" Richard sneered.

"You're in for it this year, Colin." He laughed. "You don't even know. You're in for it." The sneer twisted into a smile. "You're going to be the Grunt."

I perked up in my seat.

"Excuse me?" I said.

Richard bit his lips.

"What did you just say?" I asked.

I fixed Richard with my eyes.

"Did you just say Colin is going to be the Grunt?"

"No . . . ," Richard stammered.

"That is what you said."

"Who wants to know?" He eyed me with suspicion. "Are you one of them? You can't be. They wouldn't be caught dead hanging around with Colin."

"One of who?" I asked.

"Yeah, who wouldn't be caught dead with me?"

"Shut up, Colin," Richard and I both said at once.

Richard looked me up and down. He stood and closed the

door. He drew the blinds on the windows so we sat in the dark, silent.

"Okay," he whispered. "But you gotta promise not to tell."

I nodded seriously and said I promised. He looked at Colin. "How about you?"

"I promise." Colin was shaking inside of his shirt.

"Have either of you," said Richard, "ever heard about The Book?"

"The Book?" I said.

"Yeah." Richard nodded. "When I was in 6th grade, like you guys, everything went bad for me. See, I was a normal kid before. Everything was good. But things changed when some guys got hold of The Book."

The Book. Like what Donovan was talking about?

"They made fun of me, laughed at me, got other kids to do it. The whole class turned against me, like their goal in life was to make me miserable. The guys started calling me Grunt. I could hear them talking about me when they thought I wasn't around. The Grunt did this, the Grunt did that. We've gotta do this to the Grunt. They had some plan for me."

My heart beat faster in my chest.

"They were having secret meetings in one of the classrooms after school. One day, I hid in the garbage can to see what they were talking about."

"In the garbage can?" Colin said.

"They were ruining my life!" His face got red. "I needed to know."

"What were they talking about?" I said.

"Me. How I was coming along. How they were doing, according to The Book."

"The Book?" I said.

"The Bully Book, that's what I call it," said Richard. "Teaches you to be cool. Tells you to pick one kid. Make his life miserable."

"It tells you how to pick him," I said, not thinking.

"Yeah," said Richard. He gave me a suspicious look. "How'd you know that?"

I didn't tell him about Donovan. About how he said he didn't want me to be the Grunt. But that I fit the description. That they had no choice.

"Just guessed," I said.

"Well," said Richard, "I wish you could guess how they pick you. I can't figure it out. I was normal. I was different before all this. I was just a normal, regular kid."

Richard crushed his big fist against his eye. He rubbed his forearm across his face. It took me half a minute to realize he was pushing the tears back in.

"Anyway," Richard continued, "however The Book says to pick the Grunt, they picked me. And Colin's a littler, stupider version of me . . ."

"Shut up!"

Colin threw a bony punch. Richard caught it with his meaty hand and leaned in close.

"So this year, Colin, the Grunt . . . is you."

I stood up. Not breathing.

"Gotta get home," I said.

Colin trembled. He broke eye contact with his brother.

"But we haven't done the—"

"Forget the assignment," I said. "Forget everything, Colin. You're going to be fine this year. Just . . ." I ran my hands through my hair, trying to organize my thoughts. "I'll do it myself at home. I'm leaving."

"You need a ride."

"I'll walk, Colin," I said. "I've got to think."

I didn't give Colin or Richard another glance, and I left that stinking house.

Going Public

Once you've got your lieutenants on board with the plan, you need to get the rest of the class involved.

You need to invent a game.

A Grunt game. Something that everyone would want to play.

It needs to have clear rules and include everybody (except the Grunt, of course). Have the kids in your class hide the Grunt's things, or only talk to the Grunt in a secret language, or act like the Grunt has a disease that no one wants to catch.

These are only some ideas. Look around and you'll figure something out. Just make sure it's all about the Grunt, and make sure you're having fun.

Journal #6

Normally, a substitute teacher is cause for rejoicing.

Didn't do your homework? = It's not being collected.

Have a class book report? = Let's watch the movie.

Under most circumstances, a substitute teacher is a great thing. When isn't it? Funny you should ask.

Today we had our first weekly vocab assignment, but Mr. Whitner wasn't in school. In his place, we had a faceless, soulless sub. It was her job to make us spell and define the words on our list, one by one.

The first to go was Jason Crazypants. His word was **yonder**.

He stood up and spelled it. No one paid attention, because nobody cares how you spell **yonder**. But Jason smirked and glanced over at Adrian and Donovan.

Jason used the word in a sentence.

"**Yonder**. Over yonder field, I can see Eric Haskins's big head."

Adrian laughed first, then Donovan. The class took a second to catch on.

I tensed up in my seat. "Your face is all red!" Ruth McNealy shouted at me from the next desk over. She was laughing with the other kids.

I turned to Melody. She glared at the sub: Why wasn't this lady doing anything?

Did she not recognize my name? She had just called attendance. But her eyes glazed over. More like a Human Substitute.

Adrian Noble went next. Circumambulate: walk or go around something.

"Whenever I see Eric Haskins, I circumambulate him to avoid the smell."

Laughter. Mr. Whitner told us using the word in a sentence helps you remember its meaning. So I guess I was just playing my part in the learning process. Human Substitute stared out the window.

Donovan's word was biannually. Biannually: occurring once every two years. He avoided looking at my side of the room entirely.

"If I see Eric Haskins . . . if I only see Eric Haskins biannually, it's too much."

He stuttered through it but still got laughs. Once people

caught on to the game, no one even tried to be clever. Somebody's word was **generally** and he said, "Eric Haskins is generally stupid."

People you wouldn't expect—like quiet Ashley Dickenson and Ruth McNealy, the girl who only wears puppy shirts!—they both used their words against me. And, of course, jerks like Nick Drumme. His word was **mourn**.

"I will not mourn at Eric Haskins's funeral."

People didn't laugh as loudly at that. Pretty bad taste from a guy I never talk to.

There must have been something really interesting out the window, because Human Substitute continued to keep her brain out of the classroom as the rest of the kids hammered me. It only stopped when Melody took her turn.

"**Blissful**: a state of extreme happiness or joy," Melody said when she stood. "It would be blissful if everyone in this room would stop acting like butt-holes."

She stared directly at Jason Crazypants.

The Human Substitute yelled, "Language!"

"But—"

"Next," she said. "Next student."

Melody sat down. She turned to me. I saw the way her

lips curved into a pout. Her eyes were eyelashy and sad.

It gave me a weird feeling.

"Don't listen to them, Eric," she said. "Act like they don't even exist."

She touched my hand and my heart beat faster. For a second, I did forget they existed. Melody squeezed my wrist and looked out at the classroom. I didn't take my eyes off her.

The next person went and they didn't make an Eric Haskins sentence. Melody let go of my arm but it took me a minute to start breathing normally again.

The Human Substitute called my name and I jumped back to attention. I was one of the last ones to do a word, and ended up with **hazardous**: full of risk, dangerous.

I hoped to fight back with my word, saying something really clever—but I choked.

"Many things in this world are hazardous," I said.

And I meant it.

Dust the Target

Everyone has at least some friends, even the biggest losers. It's something you have to deal with when you're making the Grunt.

Normal classrooms are made of minigroups of friends. This is bad. There should be one friend group with one leader: you.

A person can only be the head of one group, so there should be one group.

The Grunt is the only one left out.

If the Grunt has friends, they won't be part of your group. Then there will be two groups, and that will lead to three, and four, and five, and everything will just fall apart.

So you gotta stop this thing early on. You've got to ruin the Grunt's friendships.

It's not easy to do, and it's not pretty, but it's an important part of the strategy. You need to start fights between the Grunt and his friends. Spread rumors that will cause trouble.

Once you get the Grunt's friends to leave, you need to reward them. Invite them to your lunch table, show them how much cooler life is without the Grunt. Make their lives so good that they'll never want to go back.

They'll be happy, you'll be happy, and the Grunt will be alone. It's a win-win.

Journal #7

At lunch yesterday, Melody asked me if I wanted to get together and watch a movie after school this week. I answered yes because of a combination of social starvation and being in love with her.

I leaned over to her in class this morning and asked how we were getting to her house.

Ruth McNealy, who's in the Girl Scouts with Melody, laughed behind us. I turned to see both Ruth and the puppy on her shirt smiling at me.

"Melody," I said again, "how are we getting to your house?"

"Eric . . . " Melody looked away from me and covered her face with her hand. "I can't talk about this right now."

She was speaking through her teeth. Maybe, I thought, she has a headache.

At lunch, Ruth stomped up to me, literally dragging Melody behind her. She put her hand on one hip, and a fold in her shirt made it seem like the puppy was scowling at me. The look on its face said, everyone loves puppies, but I hate losers.

"Eric," she said, and my eyes leaped back to her face. "Melody has something she needs to say to you."

"Um . . . okay." I turned to Melody. Her chin dug into her collarbone and her short brown hair hung over her eyes. Ruth elbowed her.

"You can't send me stuff like that, Eric," she said, not looking at me.

"What do you mean?"

"It's embarrassing and I don't . . . "

"What?" I said. "What did I do?"

"Eric, I just don't like you like that!" she yelled. "You can't come to my house!"

Melody got quiet and then walked away from me. I watched her leave through the big Old Side doors.

"What is she talking about?" I asked Ruth.

"Like you don't know what you did."

"I don't, Ruth—so why don't you tell me!" I shouted.

I'm not sure if it was from Melody yelling or me, but I noticed there were five lunch tables of kids staring at me.

"Melody doesn't like you like that, Eric, and she doesn't want to sit next to you in class anymore. We already talked to Mr. Whitner about it and he changed the seats."

I must have had a surprised look on my face, because Ruth told me, "Don't be shocked, Eric. You're pathetic and you're gay. Melody will never like you."

I glanced down at the puppy. It had nothing to add, but seemed to agree with what had been said.

When I got home, things became clear.

I checked Facebook and saw this in my notifications:

> Request for status as "In a Relationship with Melody Miller" denied

Oh.

Somebody hacked my account. Set my status as "in a relationship" with Melody Miller, and when she saw the request she must have thought I was saying I liked her, or that I was asking her out.

It also looks like someone posted as me on her wall, but she'd deleted whatever it was. I don't know how long it was up or how many people saw it.

What can I do? Go up to her and say I was hacked?

She obviously hates the idea of me liking her. Before, I

could just keep it a secret and everything was fine. But now the whole school probably knows about it. Should I go around to everyone saying, just so you know, I don't like Melody? That's insane.

She's made her point. She's grossed out by me.

The three of them did a pretty good job.

Donovan helped me set up my Facebook two summers ago when I didn't know what it was. I never changed my password.

There was no other damage except this: In Activities and Interests, right after reading and bike riding, someone put "Beeing a Grunt."

This proves it. They're officially out to get me. Jason, Donovan, and Adrian have a conspiracy. And I'm their Grunt.

I deleted what they wrote and changed my password, but I still didn't feel safe. Maybe there's a way to hack it again. When Donovan first heard I didn't have a Facebook account, he said, "You're barely alive if you're not on Facebook."

Well, Donovan, I'm deleting my account now.

I guess that makes me a dead man.

Lying about the Truth

If you want to make trouble for your Grunt, don't just make up lies. Work with problems the Grunt already has.

Let's say your Grunt calls some kid a moron in class and the teacher gets mad. This is a situation that you can work with.

When everyone else is at lunch, leave a note that says "moron" on the kid's desk. Everyone will think the Grunt did it and because he's the one who called the kid a moron earlier, it'll be hard to deny it.

Or if the Grunt obviously likes someone, write a love note to him or her and sign the Grunt's name. Put it in a public place where anyone can find it and embarrass them both. The Grunt will try to say he didn't write it, but nobody will believe him.

If you're always making up crazy stories about people, you'll get a reputation as a liar. It's better to lie about the truth.

Journal #8

At Colin's house, I knocked on the door. No one answered. I knocked again. Nothing. I knocked three times before I heard the lock turn.

Colin's mother opened up. The smell of boiled chicken smacked me in the face.

"Hello." I coughed, putting my wrist to my nose.

"Oh, hello . . . ," Colin's mother said. "Aaron?"

"It's Eric. Eric Haskins," I said.

"Well, I'm sorry, Eric, Colin's not home right now. He's with his father at the library."

"Out of TV time?"

"What?"

"Nothing," I said. "I actually came to see Richard. Is he home?"

"Oh. Yes he is, Aaron. I'll go get him."

She went into the house. "It's still Eric," I said. "Nothing's changed."

A minute later, Richard appeared in the doorway—his mother had forced him across their entryway to meet me, socks sliding on the tile. There was a big Band-Aid over his left eye.

"I need to talk to you," I said, "about The Bully Book."

Richard flinched. He crossed his arm over his chest and put the other hand on the Band-Aid.

"Richard," I said, "I've gotta to shake this thing. They're ruining my life, Richard. It's like how you said it would happen."

"I don't know what you're talking about," he said.

"They made me the Grunt . . . not Colin!" I tried to shove past him, but he blocked me.

Richard glared at me, wide-eyed.

"You can't be here. I can't talk to you."

His pressed his arms against my chest, and peered over my shoulder. He tried to shut the door, but I held it open with my palm. With my other hand I grabbed a fistful of arm fat and kept him in place; he was my only lead on this thing.

"Richard, what is wrong with you?" I said. His chin was buried in his chest and he spoke through his teeth.

"You can't talk to me about this anymore," he mumbled. "You got me in a lot of trouble, you moron. If they see you talking to me, they'll . . ." He trailed off.

"What?" I said. "I can't talk to you or what? I didn't get you in trouble, Richard."

He ripped himself from my grip.

"Who is they?"

The door slammed in my face.

I didn't tell on him—I didn't say anything. This is a lot bigger than Jason and Donovan and Adrian. Everything Richard said was true—there's a conspiracy of Bully Bookers. They're in every grade. They're everywhere.

And they know Richard was talking Bully Book. They did something to shut him up. That Band-Aid.

They attacked him.

But it wasn't because of me. I didn't tell anyone. There's only one explanation. When you're on a sinking ship, you always look for the wettest hole.

Colin.

First Things First

It's time to pick your Grunt.

Choosing the perfect Grunt is the one part of this plan I've put the most thought into, and it is essential that you follow my directions exactly.

The Grunt can be a boy or a girl, but you can't just pick anyone. It's not like picking some name out of a hat or even picking someone you don't like. If you don't listen to me and just want to choose whoever you think is the biggest dork or whatever, good luck, but I'm positive the rest of the plan will not wor

Journal #9

Colin, you worm. You slimy, shiny turd.

You dense, dumb piece of crap.

You've reached a level of ineptitude I've never before seen.

Con-freaking-fragulations.

Magic

By now, you should know why this book needs to stay secret. Having a book about how to rule your class will make people suspicious. That's obvious. But the way the Grunt is picked has to stay confidential.

Magicians seem powerful because nobody can figure out their tricks. But once you do know how a trick is done, it doesn't seem cool anymore.

This book is like a magic trick that gets you to the top of your class. But if people figure out how it's done, it won't work anymore. And you'll just be a loser with a book.

Worst Case Scenario: The Grunt finds the book and learns why he was chosen.

The Grunt will, of course, know he's the biggest loser in class. What's important is that he won't know why, so he can't do anything about it.

All year, I stressed about my Grunt finding out why I picked him. If he did, maybe he could change himself. It would ruin everything.

The system is almost perfect. But that is the one flaw.

Don't let the Grunt find out.

Journal #10

I spent the entire weekend watching television. 32 total hours. That's right, Greene, you near Amish, I accomplished in two days what you couldn't do in a month. I've made a fool of you.

This kid is holding out on me. Colin Greene is holding out on me!

I went up to him in school last Friday. I said, "Colin."

I said, "Colin . . . What did you do—you dumb turd?"

Maybe this is a mistake I made. A miscalculation in my approach, but I was extremely upset at this point. I'm extremely upset at all points. See, I'm victim of a conspiracy that should be targeted at Colin.

Jason, Donovan, and Adrian have made me their Grunt and I have no idea why.

Donovan says I was picked as the Grunt for a reason. If I can find that reason, I can change myself. Then maybe the Grunt will shift to somebody else. I hope that's how it works. That needs to be the way it works.

But Colin opened his big mouth and word got around that

Richard was talking Bully Book, so somebody shut him up for good. Now I've got nothing and I needed Colin to come clean.

"Tell Eric whatcha did wrong. Who did you talk to, Colin?"

"Uh . . ." Colin stared blankly at me. "I don't know what you mean."

"Don't gimme that crap, Colin!" I yelled. "Who did you tell about The Bully Book?"

"I don't know. Nobody. I mean . . . I mean, uh . . ."

Spittle was flying at me left and right. I'm dodging it, I'm putting up my sleeves for the block. But nothing was gonna stop me from getting the answer out of Colin. I could see he was lying. He was oozing guilt.

"Really, I uh . . ." He searched for an escape but I had him cornered. "I didn't . . . I didn't . . . I didn't ask anybody about it—I swear!"

"Ask anybody about it?" I said. "Who'd you ask about it?"

"No one!"

A picture formed in my mind. Colin got scared. All that talk of how he was bound to be the next Grunt. He was worried about it, who wouldn't be? But who did he turn to? There's not a person alive Colin's not afraid of.

Not that he's got good reason to be scared. The Grunt is me.

"Listen, Colin," I said, trying to calm down, "I'm not mad at you. No one's mad at you. I just want to know who you talked to. Whoever it was, it got back to Richard."

"Richard knows?" Colin asked.

"Yes, Richard knows. Whoever's in charge of all this stuff, they got to him. That's why I need to know who you talked to. I think they might be part of it."

"No, no that's not true." Colin said, looking over my shoulder.

"It is true, Colin. Now tell me who you talked to."

I leaned in close and whispered. "Who?"

"No one!" he screamed, and a bubbly wad of spit arced out of his mouth and onto my cheek.

A couple of things then happened very quickly. I'm not sure in what order.

I howl in disgust
Colin pushes past me
I lose my balance

I try to wipe my cheek with my sleeve
My fist makes contact with Colin's nose

*****

Something about the color of blood freaks people out so much that talking to them is impossible.

Even if you and another kid are just standing in the hallway saying sorry to each other, because one of you is covered in blood, everything looks insane.

So when Ms. Julie, the hall monitor who always wears a pair of yellow earphones, saw us in the hallway, the blood and whatever Stephen King audiobook she was listening to made her scream so loud the whole school heard it.

Teachers and kids came out of classrooms, janitors dropped their mops, even the hamsters in the science room, I imagine, stopped spinning in their wheels for a minute. All eyes were on Colin and me.

Colin with a bloody nose dripping onto his cruddy shirt, and me with his blood on my knuckles. Caught red-handed.

So that's how I got to learn about another one of Clark's New Rules: No Roughhousing. Requires 3-hour detention and a note from your parents.

So, thank you, Colin. You wrecked my only connection to info on The Bully Book. You got me into more trouble than I've ever had in my life. And you still haven't told me who you spilled your guts to.

You're a great study partner.

Trouble

If you use this book, you might get into trouble. But you'll know how to get out of it.

The first rule: Never get physical with your Grunt. Don't hit, trip, or touch your Grunt. Marks on the body are impossible to explain away. Use only words.

If words are what got you into trouble, then words can get you out of it.

The second rule: Always tell your own side of the story.

If the Grunt says you were making fun of him, don't call the Grunt a liar. Say he misunderstood.

Tell the teacher you and your friends were hanging out, and the Grunt started talking to you. Say that it was hard to understand the Grunt so you said, "Kid, we don't know what you're talking about." Then say the Grunt got upset about it and told a teacher you were being mean.

Say you should have been more sensitive, that you know the Grunt is kind of thin-skinned. Get your friends to back up this story.

The teacher, the principal, whoever, they're going to like this approach better than just calling the Grunt a liar. People can see right through that. Tell them you're sorry the Grunt got upset and that you'll try to be nicer in the future.

Adults want to think that everybody's nice to each other and all the bad stuff happens by mistake. None of them can remember what it's really like, and none of them can do anything about it, either.

Journal #11

"Now, I know you say it was an accident," Clark lectured me from behind his desk, "but we put ourselves into situations that allow accidents to happen."

"He spit his phlegm on me," I said back. "That's not a situation I can control!"

"Sometimes, if we're in an agitated state of mind, we do things we don't mean to. Like you bloodying Colin's nose."

"It was just an accident."

"I know," Clark said, "but it's the second time you've been in my office for 'an accident' this year."

"This has nothing to do with that," I said, looking away from him. A picture of Young Tony on vacation with his family waved at me.

"Maybe it does," he said. "A lot can change in 6th grade. It can be hard to adjust."

For a minute, I considered telling him the truth. The Evil Three, The Bully Book, all of it. But I didn't know how to say it.

The reason I peed myself is that these guys scared me.

I accidentally hit Colin because he talked to somebody about The Bully Book. In English class, everyone except Melody uses their vocab words to make fun of me. Not just a couple jerks, nearly the entire class.

It's too much to put into words, and thinking about it made my throat close up.

"And your detention form isn't signed, so I'm going to have to call your mother."

"But I came to detention," I said, coming out of it. "What does it matter if she knows or not?"

"Sorry, bud." Clark said. "That's the New Rules. This is for your well-being."

"Wait!" I pleaded. "Can't you just call my dad? He's my parent too." Mom would not understand this. I knew she would freak out. I tried to email the form to Dad's office, but he didn't write me back.

"I'm sorry, Eric. Your mother is listed as the primary guardian." Clark tried to give me a meaningful look.

"I know your parents' divorce was pretty recent. It must have been difficult when your father moved out of the country. If you ever want to talk about it . . . that's what I'm here for."

I think Principal Clark saw some TV movie called **World's Most Wonderful Principal** and based his entire life around it, because I get the feeling that everything he says and does is a giant act.

His facts aren't even right. My parents divorced 3 years ago, and my dad never left the country. He moved to Virginia because he lost his job here and that's the only place he could find work. It's not like he moved to France.

Clark held the phone to his ear and we both sat listening to the ringing over the line. When Mom picked it up, a big smile smeared all the way across Clark's face.

"Mrs. Haskins, it's Principal Clark. Very well. I'm calling about the cookies you made for the Booster Bake Sale. I'd like to order 2 dozen more!" Clark laughed. "Actually, I'm calling about Eric. He's gotten into some trouble at school . . ."

I could imagine the temperature rising in my mother's forehead over the phone. It was like a faint whistle. I imagined her eyes bulging and her face getting red.

Clark finished and hung up the phone, still smiling. "That wasn't so hard. Your mother's quite a woman."

Would he say that if she could ground him with no TV?

Clark got up to leave.

"Now just hang tight here and enjoy the ambience. Mrs. Bellemont will let you know when it's all right to leave. Good talk today."

Clark went out of the office and left me staring at a framed photograph of people jumping from an airplane with the word TRUST written underneath. If someone you TRUST has convinced you to jump out of an airplane, I suggest you rethink your relationship with them.

I just might hate this guy.

Who's in Charge?

These days, when I look at my parents, I sometimes think: Who Are These People?

'Cause when I was little, I thought Mom and Dad were like superheroes. They were smart and safe, and there wasn't a problem they couldn't solve.

Then I got to school.

It was there that I realized the world is a lot bigger than me and my family. There were teachers, hall monitors, principals, librarians, janitors, bus drivers, and kids. There were a lot of kids.

Kids that were mean to each other, and mean to me—you never knew what they were thinking. You never knew what they wanted. I couldn't figure it out and when I went to my parents for help, they couldn't either.

"Just be yourself." "Be nice to others." "Share." My parents had lots of advice for me, but no real facts about the way life worked.

That's when I realized something. They didn't understand

kids any better than I did. They just pretended to.

So I learned to depend on myself. For years, I watched how the world worked and formed the ideas in this book.

I like my parents. But I don't tell them everything, because they can't control everything.

So much in my life is up to me.

Journal #12

Whitner is gone again. Another vocab Monday in misery. I tried to zone out, so all I can remember is that Adrian Noble wishes I would **cease** to exist.

My mom is so mad about Colin Greene. She has gone insane.

She doesn't understand what's going on. But it's not like I can explain anything to her. What can you honestly say about this stuff?

When I get home from school and I'm safe from it all, the last thing I want is to relive it. Especially with my crazy mom.

She was like, "How could you do this! How could you hurt someone!"

And I tried to tell her it was complicated. I had good reasons. It was an accident.

"When is there ever a good reason to hurt someone, Eric? That's not what I taught you. That's not the son I raised!"

This isn't about the son that she raised. This is about the son who's in trouble. The son who's a target, a Grunt.

The son that she does not have the power to help.

So I started to cry a little. Fortunately, Mom misinterpreted this, as she does everything. She didn't know it was because I'm trapped in a maze of torture. She thought I was crying because I was sorry.

So to prove it, she made me call Colin and invite him over for dinner on Friday. That's right, dinner with Colin Greene. If he ends up sitting across from me, I'm wearing a smock.

When it rains, it pours.

Liars

Someone is lying to you if:

When they look into your eyes, they blink a lot.
They talk slower than usual.
When you walk into a room they immediately stop what
they're doing.
Questions bother them.
Their voice gets higher.
Their body freezes.

Journal #13

Dinner with Colin tonight.

It's all about listening carefully to the conversation. That's how you catch a crook.

MOM: So boys, what did you do in school today?

COLIN: Uh . . . not much, Mrs. Haskins.

ME: Nothing, Mom.

(This isn't entirely true. I hid from The Evil Three in the bathroom all recess, and it vastly improved my day.)

MOM: Well, you can't have done nothing. They don't have you staring at walls all day.

ME: Pretty much.

MOM: Colin. What was the first class you and Eric had today?

COLIN: That's homeroom, Mrs. Haskins.

MOM: It's Ms. Haskins, Colin. Not Mrs. Haskins.

COLIN: Oh, sorry.

(My mom is so annoying about people calling her Mrs. She might as well get a giant tattoo on her left hand that says

NO WEDDING RING! SEE!)

Mom: That's all right, Colin. Now, what did you do in homeroom? What's that class all about?

Me: Taking attendance.

Mom: All right, fine. What was the class *after* homeroom?

Colin: That's math, Mrs . . . uh, Ms. Haskins.

Mom: Math? Wonderful! You love math, Eric!

Me: English.

Mom: What?

Me: I like English, Mom.

Colin: I like math.

And that's when it hit me. Colin likes math.

Ever since he signed up for the Math Buddies program, Colin's grades in math have been getting better and better. And if you ask Colin why his math skills have improved so much (as my mother did at dinner), he'll tell you two words.

Colin: Matt Galvin.

Mom: So he's an 8th grader that you meet with?

COLIN: Yeah, I meet him once a week on . . . Wednesdays.

Gotcha, Colin. Matt Galvin is the 8th-grade Boy Scout who runs the Math Buddies tutoring program. Even though he's going for a Teach Math to Babies badge, he seems like an all-right guy. A friendly face that Colin wouldn't be afraid to approach.

It was on a Tuesday that I went over to Colin's house and Richard told us about The Bully Book. He predicted that Colin would be this year's Grunt and be tortured and humiliated. Terrified, Colin went to the biggest, coolest kid he knows, Matt Galvin, who he meets with on Wednesdays.

When my mom excused herself to go the bathroom, I grabbed Colin by the arm.

"What did Matt Galvin tell you about The Bully Book?" I said.

"Nothing," Colin stammered. "I never mentioned it to anybody."

I picked up a piece of silverware and held it under the table. I let it brush up against Colin's leg, poking him.

"This fork says you did mention it."

"Ahh!" Colin screamed. "Okay, okay! I'll tell you, just don't stab me!"

"No problem," I said, putting the utensil on the table. "It was only a spoon. Now confess."

"Okay. When Richard told us about everything, I was scared. I didn't wanna get made fun of. I hate being made fun of."

Colin hasn't had it so bad lately.

"So the next day at school, I was really nervous. I kept looking around, seeing bullies everywhere. I couldn't believe somebody would have such an evil book. I got so worried that after school I threw up."

If there isn't bodily fluid, it's not a Colin Greene story.

"I sat in the bathroom for a while just feeling awful. And then I remembered I was late for Math Buddies. When Matt asked me where I'd been, I just told him the whole thing."

"So, you told Matt Galvin about The Bully Book? About the Grunt? What did he say?"

"Well, he listened to the story. Then he looked at me and said, 'I've been a Boy Scout for a long time, so I know a lot about secret codes, and old books, and all sorts of different clubs and oaths and everything. And I've never heard of a Bully Book. And even though "Grunt" is a name you might call someone you don't like, there's no such thing as the kind of Grunt you're talking about. It's probably just

Richard's imagination. Just a crazy conspiracy theory.'"

Colin sat back in his chair. He had a satisfied look on his face.

This was trash. Clearly, Matt Galvin's words were comforting to Colin. I wish they could have comforted me. But it didn't fit the facts.

Even if there's no such thing as a Bully Book, and the stuff I heard from Richard and Donovan is wrong, and everything I've been going through is completely random, it still doesn't explain who beat up Richard and why.

Here's what I know:

- Jason, Donovan, and Adrian have all teamed up to make my life miserable.
- Donovan said I am the Grunt because I fit the description in a book that they have.
- Richard told me and Colin he was the Grunt in sixth grade when a bunch of guys teamed up against him.
- Colin told Matt Galvin that Richard was talking about The Bully Book and then Richard was beaten up.

Looking at this evidence, here's the best guess I have on what's happening:

There is a Bully Book that gets passed down from grade to grade. I'm sure of that now. It also looks like there is a group of kids in the middle school who are part of the conspiracy—they're the ones who beat up Richard. I bet they're all former Bully Bookers.

Colin told Matt Galvin that Richard was talking about The Bully Book and then Richard got beat up. Either Matt Galvin is a Bully Booker or he told some friend of his about this crazy story Richard Greene's little brother shared with him—and that friend is a Bully Booker.

Those are the only two ways the Bully Bookers in the middle school could have found out about Richard spilling it.

Either Matt Galvin is a very dangerous man—or he's in danger himself. No matter which way it is, I need to learn more about him. He's close to The Book, or at least friends with someone who is. He could get me back on track to finding The Bully Book and the reason I'm the Grunt.

We finished dinner and Colin finally went home.

There is a lot that I need to plan for. But first, Mom says I need to wash the spittle stains out of this tablecloth.

Being Myself

I've been telling you to do things differently. It's probably not what you're used to. It's not how people make friends on TV.

Everybody says to find people you can be yourself around. What they don't tell you is who "yourself" is. This never worked for me. Whenever I tried to "be myself," I could never come up with anything to say.

I think I know why this is.

You're told who you are by the people around you. People act the way they're expected to.

Everyone acts different around different friends. With some friends you're goofy, with some friends you're cool. You act different with your mom and dad than you do with your grandma.

Everyone is telling you who to be. This isn't bad if everyone expects you to be the coolest kid in class. Then, being happy and popular is easy.

But some people are expected to be losers, or idiots, or

punching bags, and because they don't know any better, that's how they act.

I did.

But not anymore. I realized being yourself isn't something that just happens. You have to create yourself. And to keep yourself safe, you have to create other people too, like the Grunt.

Make them how you want them to be.

Journal #14

I'm freaking out a little. On the bus. Trying to calm down.

The bus is shaky. It's hard to write.

I think the bus driver is eyeing me right now.

He stopped.

I snuck out of recess. I got on the preschool bus that takes home the a.m. preschoolers.

This bus will stop near the middle school.

I've got to find Matt Galvin.

I went up to a little kid waiting for the preschool bus. Told him my name was Colin Greene, that I was a school safety officer and would help him get on the bus. This kid knew nothing of Stranger Danger.

The driver asked what I was doing on the preschool bus.

The kid said I was Colin Greene, safety guy.

Now I'm on the bus.

The middle school's in my sights.

Journal #15

Middle-school recess was insane. The sun felt hotter there for some reason. Kids were screaming, running, kicking balls, swinging bats, and spinning jump ropes around their bodies like whips. If you walked too close to anybody, you'd get knocked out. They zoomed past me in all directions. Like I was stranded in the middle of a highway and trying not to get run over by the SUVs.

I had to find Matt Galvin. My watch told me there were 20 minutes until the p.m. preschool bus left for Arborland Elementary. I looked for him all over the enormous playground. It's like a city of kids. The baseball players had made a diamond out of hats and jackets, and their bats and ball were real, not the NERF kind we have. The batter cracked one hard and it flew into an angry clump of boys playing football. It hit one of them in the leg or the arm, it was hard to tell, and like a nestful of hornets, they buzzed around in a rage, charging at the baseball guys. They hurled insults and pointed fingers. I checked their faces for Matt Galvin, and just when it seemed the football and baseball kids were going to attack each other, a whistle sounded and an angry recess monitor ran between them, threatening detentions.

No Matt Galvin there, so I continued on. Past the girls practicing cheers and chasing each other in tag, and the angry kids who sat on swings without swinging, just twisting around and drawing lines in the dirt with their shoes. The sidewalk-chalk drawers, the fake-karate fighters, and the squirrel torturers all went by in a blur.

Just as I was congratulating myself for blending in, I smashed full on into a bony object. I thought I might have walked into a small tree, but when I got up, I saw a kid about my height picking himself off the ground.

"Sorry," I said. "Didn't see you there."

"Maybe that has to do with the direction your eyes were pointed," he said back. "Front way's usually the best."

He talked at me through a massive overbite but didn't make eye contact.

"Sorry," I said again.

"Oh, it happens," he said to himself, walking off. "Happens. Happens. Happens all the time."

It was then that I saw him. A blood-red ball ricocheted off the brick school building and arced in the air. Down it fell and was slammed by the fists of a blond boy giant. Matt Galvin.

He was playing wallyball by the big double doors at the back of the school. A long line of kids waited behind him and his opponent. Matt bounced a ball off the wall and it crashed into the other kid's face.

"You're out!" Matt Galvin screamed, laughing. The next in line replaced him and the game went on. I walked to the blacktop and stood behind the group. Matt's opponent tried to return a ball, but jammed his fingers and yelped in pain. The ball bounced away from the blacktop and toward the double doors.

"You idiot!" Matt Galvin yelled. "Somebody get that."

Two kids rushed to get Matt Galvin's ball. I'd seen him before, talking about Math Buddies, but he didn't look ready to teach me math just now. His blond spiky hair was like a buzz saw. His braces made him look metallic and dangerous. He was a predator—ready for the kill.

"Demolish this kid, Matt! Knock him out!" his friends called to him, and he launched the ball. His skinny opponent shivered as Matt and friends surrounded him, shouting, "Come on! Do something, you wimp! Hit it!" The way they got in his face and yelled reminded me of Jason Crazypants.

These weren't Boy Scouts. They were barbarians.

And Matt Galvin was a Bully Booker. I was sure of it.

"Hey kid, you're up!" someone shouted.

I looked around. Who was up?

"I'm talking to you, kid. You gonna play or not?"

Terror. Matt Galvin was standing five feet away from me. Piercing me with his stare. He held the wallyball in his hands.

I was next in the line. I guess I'd been standing in line to play the whole time, and moving up without noticing it. Matt Galvin stared at me with his mouth hanging open, his braces blinding me.

"Ready?" he said.

I meant to tell him no thank you. I meant to say I got in line by mistake, that the next kid should go, my leg hurt, a sprained wrist, I had homework to do, a doctor's appointment. Excuses rushed through my mind. Time slowed down. But I had to act. My brain shouted, Say something!

"Yes."

SLAM! The ball launched off the wall and a red, round flash of light targeted my face.

I think I said the wrong thing.

The ball trounced my forehead and exploded fireworks in

my eyes. I went dark and could hear the ball bouncing away.

"Dang," someone said. "Where'd it go?"

A confusion of voices, sounds. I couldn't see straight. Everything was blurry shadows. I stumbled over the blacktop.

"There it is!" someone shouted. They laughed. "It's by the Grunt."

I froze. I'd been found out. Matt Galvin had recognized me, or somebody had. Who knows how organized these people are. Maybe there's a list, or a pamphlet, a website, I don't know! But I was in dangerous territory.

"Hey, Grunt," I heard someone yell, and recognized the voice as Matt Galvin's. "Give us that ball!"

"Okay, okay," I mumbled under my breath. My vision was coming back and I grasped around my feet for the ball. I couldn't find it on the ground nearby, so I dropped to the grass and crawled. I swiped my hands around, but didn't catch anything.

"Hey, Grunt! It's right there, just pick it up and throw it back to us."

Okay, I thought. These guys are going to kill me. I had to get this ball and get out of there. But then my eyes cleared up. I could see the blood-red circle, not anywhere near me, but 50 feet off, closer to the big school doors.

I looked at Matt Galvin and his friends. None of them seemed to notice me. They all looked in the general direction of the doors, the ball, and the angry kid with the big overbite who was now picking up the wallyball. He held it in two hands, like you would a basketball, and gave one of the worst tosses I've ever seen in my life.

It didn't fly more than 10 feet before dropping to the ground. Matt and his friends laughed and one of them ran to pick it up. The bony kid walked away, mumbling to himself.

The 8th-grade Grunt. They'd been yelling at him. Matt Galvin was the 8th-grade Bully Booker, and this weirdo the 8th-grade Grunt. I'd lost Richard, but I'd found him.

Just as I was making my way over to tell him we were the same, Grunts of different generations, the alarm buzzed on my watch. I was late. If the preschool bus back to Arborland El wasn't at the middle school already, it would be soon, and the stop was a football field away. I had to run.

With a quick glance back, I memorized this Grunt's face before racing to the stop.

I arrived back in school just in time to have a perfectly miserable day.

Journal #16

The bus didn't get me back from the middle school in time for class, so I had to come up with an excuse for where I was. I went with an old standby: bathroom problems.

When I told Whitner this, he gave me a serious look and then talked for 8 minutes about his personal history with "bathroom problems" and strategies to deal with them. I now know more than I ever wanted about Mr. Whitner's intestines.

I don't know if I can get away with sneaking into the middle school again.

That's why I went to the library and searched their School History section—basically a foot and a half of shelf space that holds old yearbooks and stuff. I pulled out the 2010 edition.

It was weird seeing all the kids that used to go here. I saw middle schoolers I recognized from the playground, but younger, wearing sweaters and goofy haircuts. Even Matt Galvin and his friends were in there, and they all looked so normal. Just regular kids dressed up for their yearbook photos. You would never guess that these 6th graders were making some kid's life miserable.

This kid—Daniel Friedman. The one with the overbite, the 8th-grade Grunt. Calling him my ancestor is one way of looking at it.

I was half expecting a name like Dillmount Finster, or Tristan Fjord, something Gruntlike. But I guess Eric Haskins is pretty normal too.

You're given your name for no reason; your mom and dad just make it up. But you don't become the Grunt for no reason. There's a formula. It's something you do, or something you are. If I could figure out what it is about me, I could change it. And maybe then I wouldn't be the Grunt anymore.

'Cause it lasts past 6th grade. You can see it in guys like Richard, and this Daniel kid. You don't stop going to school with your bullies. They only get bigger.

Something I've been thinking about is, if I get to know this Daniel Friedman kid, maybe I could do some sort of comparison, like a checklist between him, Richard, and myself, and see what we all have in common. I could isolate the Grunt trait, get rid of it, and then the position will shift to somebody else. At least that's how I hope it would work. I don't know what else I can do at this point.

Donovan said it's not personal. He said he didn't want to choose me, but there's a formula. It's something about me. He said it wasn't up to them to decide. I know because I wrote it down right after I heard him say it.

I'm glad I did, 'cause otherwise I might not have remembered something that important. I've been carrying my notebook around with me everywhere lately. I'm using it as a sort of a case journal, a place to write down events and conversations, anything that I could use as a clue.

I just picked up the district directory from the librarian at the front desk. It has the phone numbers and addresses of every student in the Arborland School Ditrict. Now that I've got Daniel Friedman's name, I've got his number and his address.

I think it's about time I pay him a visit.

Not All Bad

My Grunt hates me. But I'm actually making his life easier.

I put an incredible amount of thought into every social decision I make. The same goes for most of the kids in my class.

Who do I sit with at lunch? Is this person mad at me? Think I'm cool enough? What should I say to her? How do I avoid him?

Life is not easy in sixth grade.

Every choice you make might be a wrong one and you can never go back. But my Grunt never has to make any hard choices at all.

I'm constantly on top of my game, playing kids off each other, working things to my advantage, all so I can get what I want. It's exhausting.

But my Grunt never gets what he wants, so he can just relax.

He doesn't need to worry about what he'll say or do in

class, because he'll get made fun of no matter what. He doesn't need to worry about making friends, because I've made sure that's not possible.

In the beginning, he tried to fight it, but he got the picture after a month or two. The best advice I could give to any Grunt would be:

Relax. Enjoy the lack of choices.

Don't fight it.

Journal #17

Daniel's house isn't far from my school and the middle-school kids get out later than us, so I had time to set up shop.

See, I didn't want to go into this lightly. After what happened to Richard, I'm only going to bring this Bully Book stuff up with the right guy. I was 99 percent positive Daniel was the Grunt, but I had to make sure. I waited in the bushes by his house until I heard someone coming down the road—talking to himself. I saw him in a lime-green sweatshirt, just a few feet away from me. I sucked in air till my spine curved and launched my attack.

"HEY, GRUNT!"

For one kid every year, that word is like a dog whistle. Daniel passed my test. He froze, his shoulders tensed, his neck shot up like a periscope, sucking in the sights for Bully Bookers. He was a Grunt all right, and he bolted before I could explain myself.

I was plowing after him, my sneakers slapping the pavement. "Wait!"

He slipped into the forested area behind the houses and I saw him tripping down the woody hill to the ravine. We were in thick jungle now, tree branches everywhere, ready to poke your eyes out. I could see a green flash between the leaves and I followed it fast. I raced through the tree trunks, right on the edge of falling over if I didn't keep my speed. I felt something hit my toe and then I was tumbling down the hill. My face tasted a gnarly root and my hair soaked up mud. The earth was spinning around—punching at me from all angles.

I landed in something wet. I was at the bottom of the hill and had trouble standing up. "Daniel," I called out weakly. "Daniel!"

I waited for the spinning to end.

A flash of green.

There! Under a branch, some ways off in the distance.

He was holding something with both hands. There was a pop. It was a gun.

The bullet hit my chest at the bottom of my ribs. I grabbed at it and felt wetness. My chest and hand were dripping red.

The second bullet hit my back, right in the spine.

Paralyzed, I thought. I reached around to the wound and my hand came back to me . . . blue.

Paintballs.

I spun to my feet, but Daniel was gone. The sting was killer.

I knew Daniel wouldn't like me calling him Grunt, but I guess I'd underestimated him. It took all my energy just to get out of the woods and back to the neighborhood.

So the plan backfired. But I still think I can learn something from him about the Grunt.

I wrote him a message.

> Daniel, I'm sorry I snuck up on you like that. It was stupid of me. I am a friend. In fact, we've met once before, at the middle school. I got your name from the yearbook and your address from the district directory. I should have been more direct.
>
> I'm a 6th grader, and I believe I'm in a similar situation to the one you found yourself in during 6th grade. If you follow me. I need to talk to you about The Book. Please contact me.

I added my address and phone number, folded my message, and placed it in his mailbox. I hope he gets it before his mom does.

Luckily I got home before my mom did and it gave me time to get the (washable, thank God) paint out of my clothes.

The ball's in Daniel's court now. I'm going to bed.

Journal #18

Outside the classroom windows today, the snow came down for the first time—but nobody even got up out of their seats to look.

The class was buzzing with talk. The Human Substitute even broke her daze to tell people to stop whispering. Nobody told me what was going on, of course, but I did hear Ruth McNealy say, "and now they're going out with each other" to Ashley Dickenson as they came into homeroom.

I was pretty shocked when I heard it. Beyond embarrassing me on Facebook, I didn't know kids were actually dating yet. I don't have any regular friends, how can I be expected to get a girlfriend?

I figured it had to be someone in our class because everyone was passing around notes. It's like they all grew up overnight, and everyone knew what to do.

I wanted somebody to tell me what was going on, so I wrote a note to the one guy I thought would respond to me, Colin Greene.

What's going on today?
Who's going out with who?

Colin perked up and started squirming in his seat. He held my note in the air like a miner who'd just found gold. He's probably never gotten one before.

He spun around and his eyebrows were dancing on his head with excitement. I nodded to say, The note's from me.

"I know, Eric, I know!" Colin whispered a little too loud. "I heard it on the bus today!"

I gestured for Colin to lower his voice, but he was so excited to have some gossip that he couldn't keep from shouting.

"You'll never believe it!"

"Quiet down there," the Human Substitute said. "Time for Vocab Words now."

Whitner's been gone just about every Monday this year. We always get the Human Substitute and Vocab Words always goes the same.

Adrian Noble said you'd need to suspend disbelief to think that I wasn't gay. Donovan said my head was as big as a monument. Nick Drumme got the word **photosynthesize**. He didn't really know what to do with it. But he said plants photosynthesize their food about as well as I make myself look like a gaywad. Which I thought was pretty creative.

The weird moment came with Jason Crazypants. His word was perfect. A gift from the bullying gods. **Imbecile**: someone of low or below-average intelligence.

I tightened my grip on the desk and got ready for "Eric Haskins is an imbecile." I cursed the vocab-list-making people for including that one.

Jason stood up, cleared his throat, and glanced at Adrian Noble. He looked at his feet, and then over to Melody. She gave him a quick nod.

"Someone who cannot pass fifth-grade English is an imbecile." He coughed and sat down.

I leaned back in shock. Everything was laid out perfectly. Eric Haskins is an imbecile. He spared me, and didn't make fun of anyone else, either. That's not the Jason I know and hate.

He smiled at Melody and that made me suspicious. When Colin explained to me what he'd heard, it nearly broke my heart.

*****

Jason told Melody he liked her over the weekend. She asked him to give her some time to think about it. The next day, she said she would date him on one condition: that he stop being mean to people.

It doesn't make sense to me. Melody hates Jason just as much as I do. She obviously knows he's a jerk, or why else would she make him promise that?

I can't believe she brought me into this—I'm the only one Jason's mean to nowadays. She probably thinks she's protecting me. I don't want this kind of protection.

And could someone please explain to me why she was so embarrassed when she thought I liked her, but when Jason asks her out, she says yes?

Because he's cool and I'm the Grunt. That's all there is to it.

The Bully Book works.

And it's smarter than you, Melody.

While Colin was telling me about their unholy union, Jason and Adrian came up to us in the hallway. As they passed, Crazypants grabbed the strap of my backpack and pulled me close to him. Melody wasn't around. He put his mouth to my ear and said, "By the way: Eric Haskins is an imbecile."

He checked me against the bricks. Jason and Adrian walked away, laughing. Colin and I just stared at each other, not saying anything.

Working the Class

You need to remember that this is about happiness. About making the world better for yourself and the kids in your class. So everyone should see you as a pretty nice person.

The Grunt's gonna hate you; there's nothing you can do about that. But make sure that everybody else loves you. Even if that means that you just act like a kid they can love.

If you're getting a reputation as a mean person, you're not doing this right. There's a balance between putting the Grunt in his place and being a leader in the classroom.

It's all about appearances.

Journal #19

I don't like being me anymore.

When I write "anymore" it makes it seem that there was a time I did like being myself. But that's not what I'm saying.

It's not like I was this kid who looked in the mirror every morning and shouted, "I love myself, and it's gonna be a great day!"

Instead I thought, I want Cheerios for breakfast. I didn't think about me at all. And I never thought about liking myself or not.

I always considered myself normal. Nothing bad, nothing good.

But now, it's clear to me. I don't like myself.

Not my face, my hair, my nose, the dark circles under my eyes, the bushy eyebrows. I've got thick thighs, skinny arms, and a big round butt. I hate my voice, the way that I talk, the things I say. I hate the thoughts I think. I'm not really good at anything, and I'm not even funny. I act like I am, but really I'm not. There are a ton of people way funnier.

And I'm mean. I feel like I'm kind of mean to Colin, even though people are mean to me.

I wanna change myself. I don't wanna keep on being this person. I don't want to be the Grunt.

Journal #20

I was staring at some homework and it's math, which I am good at, but not when I'm brain-dead. And I'm currently brain-dead.

Just then I heard a crack at my window. I spun around. Another crack and I saw a rock bang against the glass. Then a bigger rock. It rattled the window.

What is going on?

I threw open my window and stuck my head out. A dark figure was running into the night.

"Hey!" I yelled.

On my front lawn I found a rock wrapped in paper. I unwrapped it and saw there was a note.

Maybe you'll learn now not to ambush me. I'm not someone you want to mess with, and I have paintballs specifically formulated not to wash out.

But you did write to me about The Book. That makes me curious, but a bit suspicious, too.

This Friday at midnight, you will come to my house alone. Look in my mailbox. You will find further instructions there.

Until then —Daniel Friedman

Journal #21

Daniel's hideout is just the kind of crazy house where you would expect a heavily armed Grunt freak to hole up in the middle of the woods. That is, if you would ever expect something like that.

In the mailbox in front of his house I found a blindfold with a note that read WEAR ME. In a few seconds, everything was pitch black and I felt a paintball gun in my ribs. "Walk," a voice commanded.

We marched for 20 minutes and I knew we had gone into the woods because I felt the snow and twigs under my boots. "Here," the voice said, and I stopped marching. My blindfold came off and I saw we were in front of a tree house somewhere in the forest.

This must have been where Daniel grabbed the paintball gun from during our previous chase. It looked like it was set up for war.

"Welcome to my fortress," Daniel said to me in the dim light of an oil lamp. The flame threw shadows of paintball guns and ammunition crates against the walls. "I make sure to prepare for anything now."

Daniel made me tell him what I knew about The Book. He made me explain how I'd spotted him as the Grunt. I told him the story of Richard Greene and of Adrian Noble, Jason Crazypants, and Donovan. I said how Colin had blabbed about The Book and why I got interested in Matt Galvin. He scowled at the name.

"Matt Galvin." Daniel spit on the floor of his tree fortress. "I hate him."

It was past midnight and very cold outside. The moon shone a strange yellow through the pine trees.

"Are you afraid of him?" I asked.

Daniel gave me a sour look. What a stupid question. I saw how he'd acted when Matt taunted him in school, and the way he panicked when I called him Grunt.

"If you think I ran away from you because I was afraid," Daniel said, "then you're wrong. I was only trying to lead you into the woods, where I could come here and defend myself. No one ambushes me anymore."

"They came to you at your house?" I said. I didn't know the Bully Bookers did that. I hoped they didn't.

"Only once," Daniel said, sighing. He looked out the

crudely cut window.

"What happened?" I said.

Daniel stared at me grimly. "You're chasing The Book?" he said. "What would you do if you had it?"

"Read it," I said. "See why I was picked for the Grunt and change. I'd change myself so I didn't fit the description. So I wouldn't be the Grunt anymore."

"That's what I should have done," Daniel said, "when I had it."

I jumped up off the floor. "What?" I shouted. And Daniel told me his story:

His 6th-grade year had been a lot like mine: a normal and pretty boring existence destroyed by three kids he'd known since kindergarten. The leader of the gang was Matt Galvin, and soon the whole class was following in his footsteps, making Daniel's life a terror. Like me, he'd picked up hints that something more might be going on. His Bully Bookers were always sneaking out together during lunch, and it felt like there was a conspiracy against him. One time, to terrorize Daniel, Matt Galvin pulled him into the handicapped bathroom and, using a stolen janitor's key, locked him there. He'd done this kind of thing before, but this time, he made a mistake. Matt left his own backpack locked inside the bathroom with Daniel.

It was a Friday, and Daniel was afraid of being trapped over the weekend. He opened Matt's backpack, hoping to find a cell phone he could use to call for help, but when he unzipped it, he found a leather-bound binder with THE BOOK stenciled onto its cover. Just as Daniel opened it, Matt burst through the door. He ripped The Book from his hands. Daniel bolted from the bathroom, ran down the hall, and escaped the school. Matt Galvin chased after him. Daniel slipped into the woods and hid there for hours, waiting him out and reading the strange sheet of paper he'd accidentally torn from The Book.

He headed back to his house in the dark. When Daniel told this part of the story, he seemed very upset.

A strange boy appeared out of the darkness and put his hands on his shoulders. "Are you the Grunt?" he whispered. Daniel had never seen this boy before. He looked about 13 years old, tall, with dark hair covering his eyes.

"You have something that doesn't belong to you," the boy said. "Something very dangerous. Keep it, and I promise . . .

you will get hurt." The boy was cold and serious, and he looked strong. "Give it to me, and I can make sure you won't be harmed. Refuse, and I can't be held responsible for what happens."

Too terrified to argue, Daniel handed the crumbled page of The Book to the mysterious boy. Then the boy grabbed him by his shirt collar.

"You forget about this now," he said. "If you know what's good for you. You never saw The Book, and you never saw me."

And just like that, he was gone. Daniel's Bully Bookers never mentioned the incident with The Book or the stolen page again.

But, of course, after that—they made Daniel's life much worse.

"I can't believe you had a page of The Bully Book!" I shouted.

"I didn't know what it was," Daniel moaned.

"What did it say?"

Daniel sagged to the floor. His voice dropped to a whisper. "That's just it. I can't remember."

The whole experience had been too terrifying.

"The page just said something about being a manual on how to be cool. That's honestly all I know. It was the first page of the book."

"And the boy who ambushed you. You've got no idea who he was?" I said.

No wonder Daniel freaked out when I jumped him.

"I don't know. Never wanted to know."

"He's got to be a Bully Booker. For all we know, he's the kid who wrote it," I said. "You tear out a page and this old guy shows up. He might be the head of the whole organization."

"Maybe," Daniel said.

"You don't care about this? If he's the author, we've got a key to the whole thing!"

"Hey, I came when you mentioned The Book, didn't I?"

"Yeah, but this is something bigger. We've got to get a name on him."

"Look," Daniel said, rubbing his eyes. "I don't want to play detective here. I have enough trouble just going to school with these guys. I'm on defense only."

"Maybe that works for you," I said, "but this isn't over

for me. I've got half of 6th grade left to go, and I don't want it to be miserable."

"Not like it stops after 6th grade."

"Then help me," I said. "If I bring you some yearbooks, can you pick out this guy? If he's the author of The Book, that might get me closer to reading a copy."

Daniel squinted hard at me; the moon cast weird shadows on his face.

"Yeah . . . okay," he said. "But I don't want you to contact me anymore. News travels fast with these guys, and I don't want anything happening to me like it did with Richard Greene."

"You heard about that?" I said.

"Hard to miss." Daniel pointed to his eye where Richard got punched. "So here's what you can do. Photocopy your yearbooks and put them in my mailbox. I'll look through the pictures and get a name back to you somehow. That sound good?"

"Yeah, Daniel," I said. "Thanks."

"No, thank you," he said.

"For what?"

"For being polite enough to do this again."

Daniel held up the blindfold. He led me through another dark walk over muddy ground. 20 minutes later, we stopped and I took it off. I was standing on the street in front of my house, and Daniel was gone.

Maintenance

If this book is going to last, you'll need to take care of it.

Fix holes in the paper so they don't fall out of the binder.

Get new metal rings when they stop snapping into place.

Retype pages that are getting hard to read—do it accurately.

Burn old pages that are being replaced. DO NOT LEAVE THESE AROUND.

Don't get lazy about this.

Journal #22

It was nearly a week ago that I gathered up the photocopies I'd made of 5 years' worth of yearbooks (all the school library had) and stuffed them into Daniel Friedman's mailbox. Tonight a single page wrapped around a rock has come back to me.

On that page are the smiling faces of nearly thirty 6th graders, all in 10th grade now, all of them probably forgetting the torture they made for one of their classmates, the Grunt, who I can't pick out from these photos alone. None of them remembering what they did, except maybe one. The boy with dark hair hanging low in front of his eyes. The one with the big red circle markered around his picture. Daniel Friedman's ambusher. The oldest Bully Booker that I know of. Maybe the Author himself.

Clarence Corbinder.

Journal #23

Clarence's house has a dead look. Even worse 'cause winter's hit hard. Dirty snow's piled up along the street edges.

It's a pretty large house, bigger than mine and very modern, with huge gray aluminum walls. Sort of like living in a large sardine can. The only thing that doesn't look clean and lifeless are the basement windows. They stick up at the ground level and are plastered with newspaper. Like someone doesn't want you knowing what goes on down there.

I pulled Clarence's address out of the school directory, and it took me about half an hour to get up the courage to approach the side of his house. Seemed like nobody was home. Except there was a light on in the basement. You could see it shining through the newspaper.

See, I'm not sure if Clarence knows I exist or not. Say he is the author of The Bully Book, or even just high up in the organization. Would he know about me? Do the Bully Bookers in high school keep up with each year's 6th-grade Grunt?

I don't think he's seen me in person before, but I haven't seen him, either, and there I was at his house. He could use a yearbook and a phone directory just as easily as I could. I spotted a shadow moving against the newspaper. Somebody was down there.

"Excuse me!"

I spun around and covered my face with my hand. Through my fingers, I saw a woman, 40-ish, with big hair and an expression like she was holding in a fart and enjoying it.

"Can I help you?" the woman asked. I froze, not knowing what to do. Was this Clarence's mom? Even the author of The Bully Book has a mother.

"Uh . . . Mrs. Corbinder?" I said.

"Yes. That's me." She smiled. "What are you doing at my house, young man?"

"Um . . . me?" I tried to catch my breath.

"Yes, you. What's your name, son?"

"My name, that's . . ." I couldn't give her my real name; what if she mentioned it to Clarence? I couldn't have him knowing I was there. "It's Colin Greene, ma'am. My name is Colin Greene."

Mrs. Corbinder gave me a smile. "Well, Colin. What are you doing wandering around my backyard?"

I tried to think of something other than, *I'm checking out your house for weak points so I can break into it and steal a book that your evil son has.*

But Mrs. Corbinder chimed in for me, "Oh, you must be looking to shovel the walk! Well, I'll tell you, I'll need it. The weatherman says we've got about 10 inches of snow coming down next week, and my Clarence is just about as lazy as a sack of potatoes! Spends all his time down in the basement doing his homework or God knows what else!" She laughed, almost manically.

And that's how I got a job keeping the driveway and sidewalks clear at the Den of Evil. I'll be back when the big storm hits. When I'm shoveling, I'll really be checking the house for a way inside. And when I find one, I'll break in and take that awful book.

Journal #24

Principal Clark is a phony. He's a fraud. He called everyone into the auditorium to do a speech about school violence. Trying to scare us so that nobody brings a Swiss Army knife to school "Or it's a 180-day suspension." Another one of his New Rules. Zero Tolerance is what they call it.

Zero Tolerance is what I have for him right now. He wasted our time, calling the whole school together. And he told us not to bring knives. For our own safety. Who does he think is bringing knives to school?

Nobody. If he had half a brain, he'd be talking about the things that can really hurt you here. Like other freaking kids.

No one in my class was paying attention. They were whispering to each other.

I heard what they were saying: Where are Jason and Melody?

They weren't there.

"I know where they are!" said Ruth McNealy. She giggled

with a group of Melody's new friends, girls she's been hanging out with since she started dating Jason.

"They're kissing," I heard her whisper.

I felt my stomach twisting in a knot. Or like a rock was dropped in there. Or like I was going to throw up.

Everything is moving so fast. Everything's changed so much. There's nothing I can control, nothing I can do. Everyone is growing up and leaving me behind.

I can't stand all this change. I can't stand all this awfulness. Nothing's good anymore. Nothing's freaking good.

I don't want to be stuck like this forever. I don't want to be a Richard or a Daniel. I don't even wanna be Eric anymore, for God's sake. I just want to change. I don't want to be the Grunt.

I gotta get to work, and I gotta get serious.

Dating

I have a girlfriend now, even though I don't want one. There really is no point. Girls our age won't kiss you—it's not like on TV. A girlfriend is good for making a ridiculous amount of gossip in the class. That's why I have one.

It's not as if I like the girl I'm dating. She's extremely boring and dumb. But being the first in the school to have a girlfriend is special.

Everybody in sixth grade wants to seem older than the other elementary kids. Nobody can wait to grow up, even though growing up sucks as far as I can tell. So everyone thinks it's a big deal if you start "dating" someone. It makes you seem cool. Makes you seem like you're ahead of the curve. Like you're number one.

And that's the best reason to do it.

Journal #25

I dug the Corbinder manor out of 10 inches of snow on my first visit, and afterward Mrs. Corbinder invited me in for some cocoa. There was no sign of Clarence except for the lights in the basement.

As we walked inside, I noticed the differences between Clarence's house and Colin's. Instead of being a pigsty, this place was like a museum. At Colin's house, I didn't want to touch anything because it was gross. At Clarence's I didn't want to mess anything up. Guess that's the difference between being a Grunt and a Bully Booker.

"Shoes! Shoes!" Mrs. Corbinder shouted at me as I crossed inside. "Colin, this is a no-shoes house!"

"Sorry," I said, and kicked my boots off. There was hardly any furniture in the place. Just two long couches that stretched all the way across the walls. The house was very bright inside, but I couldn't tell where the light was coming from—there were no light bulbs anywhere.

"Where's Clarence?" I tried to ask causally.

"Oh, I'd imagine he's where he's always at. Down in the basement." She laughed.

"What does he do down there all the time?" I asked.

"Oh, homework. Writing things," she said.

"Writing things?"

"Oh, yes. Always writing in notebooks down there. Has stacks of paper everywhere. Never shows anything to me, though." She did that weird laugh again. "Have you met Clarence? I can call him up if you like, but I don't think he'll come. Never usually leaves the basement till dinnertime."

"No, no, that's okay," I said. I wasn't in too much of a hurry to meet Clarence, not even under a fake name. What if he recognized me?

Still, I knew I needed to get into that basement. He was the author of The Bully Book, all right. His mother had practically told me so: He's writing in notebooks all the time, has stacks of papers everywhere. Probably working on more Bully Books, maybe a high-school edition. He must have a copy of The Book stashed down there. I just needed a way to get in when no one's around.

As Mrs. Corbinder and I talked, I noticed the security system. Alarms and sensors everywhere. There'd be no way to break in during the day when the house was empty, or the middle of the night.

I had prepared for this. If you can't sneak in when no

one's home, you've got to do it when they're distracted. And I had found the perfect excuse when I was looking into Clarence's personal information.

"I hear that Clarence's 16th birthday is coming up," I said.

Mrs. Corbinder passed the cocoa. "We're having a party for him here at the house."

Bingo.

"That's great," I said. "I love birthday parties."

"Well then, uh . . ." Mrs. Corbinder was trapped; no mother can turn down an 11-year-old boy inviting himself to a party.

"You should come," she said with a forced smile.

"Really?" I said. "Oh man—that would be great!"

"Of course, Colin. It'll be wonderful to have you. The more the merrier."

And so I've got my date. In exactly 23 days, I'll be attending Clarence Corbinder's birthday party, the author of The Bully Book. And during all the distraction of the party, I'm sneaking into his basement and ending this thing, once and for all.

Journal #26

Today in English class, Whitner had us learn about public speaking. He put a bunch of topics into a hat and then made us stand in front of the class, pick one out, and talk about it for 60 seconds.

We had to make the speech up on the spot.

Ruth McNealy went first and I swear she was nearly in tears. Her topic was "What would the world be like if cars could fly?"

I don't know what Whitner was thinking.

For 60 seconds she coughed and stalled and tried to think of something to say other than she'd get to school a lot faster. The same went for Ashley Dickenson when she had to talk about "What if potato chips were good for you?" and Nick Drumme when he was told to describe a world where "Gravity is reversed."

"Come on, guys," Whitner said, "this is supposed to be fun. Just loosen up and talk." Easy for him to say; when you're the teacher, no one makes fun of you when you say something stupid. At least not to your face.

"Eric Haskins." Whitner called my name. "You're next, buddy."

"Get up there, buddy." Jason Crazypants whispered to me. Adrian Noble chuckled.

I just had to get through this. I'd say my stupid speech, they'd all laugh at me, and I'd get on with my quiet life.

Whitner held the hat and I silently cursed him for making me do this. I read my topic.

"What if people didn't have any thumbs?"

Whitner started his stopwatch. I looked at the class; they'd make fun of me no matter what I said, so why worry about it? I just told them what the world would be like, straight up.

"First, Roger Ebert would be out of a job," I said. "He'd give good movies one mangled knuckle up.

"And playing basketball, everybody'd be like, 'Hey man, high four!'"

Melody sat in the front row and broke into a high giggle.

"There'd be no more rules of thumb. Humans and monkeys would have nothing to brag about. Video games would be impossible to play and babies would be sucking on their fingers, which probably isn't nearly as satisfying."

I didn't think the jokes were that funny, but the whole class was roaring with laughter, led by Melody, who was the loudest of all. Whitner stopped the clock. He made the class clap for me like he did for everyone, but pulled me aside before I sat down. "That was really excellent, Eric," he whispered. "You've got real talent as a speaker."

Yeah, I thought, I guess I do. I turned a class of bloodthirsty savages into my friends for a minute. They liked my jokes. I looked over at Melody, who was smiling at me. She looked proud.

As I made my way back to my seat, I heard Adrian Noble talking to Ruth.

"Eric Haskins can be funny when he wants to be." He smiled.

"Yeah," she said.

"Thanks!" I said behind Ruth's back.

She froze and her shoulders tensed up like a spider had just touched her neck. Ruth turned to me slowly with a look of disgust on her face.

"Hey, get yourself outta here, Grunt," Adrian said.

Ruth fake-shivered and laughed.

I went to my seat.

I could always be like that, I thought, but you won't let me. I could be funny and nice and have friends, but they want me trapped for some reason.

"That was pretty good." Jason Crazypants leaned over his desk. "But I'm glad we still have thumbs"—he pinched my arm—"and Grunts."

Journal #27

Dad came to visit for the weekend. I'd been looking forward to it for a while, but it didn't end up being what I expected.

We went to Battle Creek to tour the cereal factory, just the two of us. Dad likes to go to places like this and I just sort of watch him have a good time.

But we didn't talk like we used to, or at least I didn't. He asked me a lot of questions. I didn't really give him good answers.

He asked me how things were at school. If anything interesting was going on. "What do you mean by interesting?" I asked.

"I don't know," he said. "Did you learn anything really mind-blowing or did anything really funny happen in class?"

"Don't think so." I said. "We're just working on math. I don't think anybody in my class is really funny."

"Do you have any teachers that you hate?"

"No," I said. "Just Mr. Whitner, my English teacher. And I don't hate him, I just don't like that he's absent every

Monday. I don't like the sub they give us."

I waited for my dad to ask why, and thought about what I'd say if he asked me. I didn't know if I'd tell him the truth.

"But he's a good teacher other than that?"

"Yeah, he's all right." I thought about the time he helped me during the Bathroom Disaster. If my dad asked me what I liked about him, is that what I'd say? Would I tell him about what's been going on this year?

"What about fights at school? Anybody being stuffed into lockers?" My dad chuckled.

"What?" I said.

"You know, kids gang up on someone, they push them into a locker?"

"No," I said. "That kinda stuff doesn't happen."

I felt queasy. My dad doesn't understand how it works, I thought. You don't get locked into lockers and robbed of your lunch money. It's nothing like on TV. It's a lot worse and a lot harder to explain to somebody who has obviously never experienced it. Because that's the only way you could laugh at that kind of stuff, Dad.

I sat in silence the next 60 seconds, wondering if Dad

would keep questioning me. What if he said, "Are kids mean to you? Do they make fun of you? Lie about you? Have they hurt you?" I didn't know what I would say.

I decided I'd tell him the truth.

If he asked me, I wouldn't lie.

I wouldn't tell the whole story at first. It'd be too hard to get out. But if he asked, "Are they mean to you?" I'd say yes. That'd lead to more questions and more questions and more, until the whole horrible year was out and in the open.

I waited, holding my breath, ready to tell him the whole thing if he asked me.

"Do you need to use the restroom?" he said.

I looked over at him slowly and shook my head no.

"Okay, 'cause the last stop for a half hour's coming up. I want to catch the news now."

He turned on the radio, and I sat there listening while the man from the news told me and my dad about stuff more important than us.

Two of Me

My school self and my family self.

At school, I am in control of what people know about me, how they see me, and how we interact.

My family knows me from a less intelligent time. They knew me before I figured life out, and they will always see me as a little kid.

I've got my kingdom at school and that's enough. My aunts can treat me like a baby and my uncles can think I'm a weakling. There's nothing I want from them anyway. When we have family dinners, I'm thinking about the clock.

But you will have a problem when family and school friends mix. Put a sick person near a healthy person. Does the sick one get healthy? Of course not, the healthy person gets sick. I don't want the way my family treats me to catch on with my friends.

So I never let them mix.

You shouldn't either.

Journal #28

Today was Clarence's birthday. I told my mom I was going to the library and biked to his house. It still had that dead look, even with 15 cars parked out front and the sound of music coming from the inside. Newspapers were still taped to the basement windows. Only one of them had a Happy Birthday sticker on it.

An older lady answered the door. "Party's inside," she said, and I followed her in.

"Colin!" a woman's voice called behind me. "Colin Greene!" I turned and remembered that I was using a fake name. Ms. Corbinder came up to me with a tray of strangely shaped cookies. "Thanks for coming, have a treat!" She was dressed in what I could only describe as a giant black bedsheet that wrapped around her body. "Have you seen Clarence yet?" She wore a demented grin.

"No, I haven't had a chance," I said.

To tell the truth, I'd been hoping to avoid the kid.

"Oh, I'll go get him, then." Ms. Corbinder clutched my shoulders with both hands. "Stay right here."

She disappeared into the blur of the partygoers, and I had to act fast. Stick to the plan: Get in, get out.

I tossed my present on the table with the rest and started searching for the entrance to the basement. People were all around me, blocking my view with their heavy sweaters and drinks in their hands. All adults on the first floor; the kids must have been upstairs. I wondered which Bully Bookers might be there, The Evil Three?

Then the bony elbows and painted fingernails cleared and a path opened up. I could see a gray doorway at the other end of the house. I gripped the key-chain flashlight in my pocket.

The basement.

Stairs creaked as I went down, and I gave thanks for the loudness of the party. The key-chain light barely brightened the darkness.

I couldn't see more than a foot in front of my face. All I could make out was brown, dirty carpeting, an old chair, and a beat-up desk. No papers. Nothing.

I cursed myself for doing this. What had I expected to find down here, anyway? A handwritten copy of The Bully Book just lying on the floor?

It was then that I hit the cabinet.

An enormous filing cabinet with two double doors. Inside were drawers and drawers packed with rows of papers. My flashlight passed over it all, crumpled notebook leaves, ink-jet-printer papers, school book reports, and personal notes like what kids would pass each other in class. They seemed to have been written by a bunch of people, not just Clarence. I flipped through the drawers and pages madly, trying to find something close to what Daniel had described. The Book.

There were ten drawers and I yanked them all open. I rummaged through each one as fast as I could, and when I determined it was junk, I slammed it shut. Who is this guy and why does he have all these papers? Was this stuff for The Bully Book? Where's the connection?

My flashlight dimmed to a glow, then went out completely. It was pitch black and here I was: in the belly of the beast.

I shuffled my way toward the stairs. Something snagged my foot and I tumbled over the rickety chair. I fell on the desk and heard its leg snap. I scrambled to stand it back up in the dark. The leg hung by a splinter of wood. As I straightened it, I felt a drawer in the desk that I hadn't seen. A secret drawer. Inside was a smooth springy sheet of 8½ x 11 laminated paper. I grabbed it and rushed up the basement stairs. On the final step, some light was leaking in from the party. I read the page:

How to Make Trouble without
Getting in Trouble, Rule the School,
and Be the Man

The Bully Book! That first page that Clarence strong-armed from Daniel!

I folded it up and jammed it in my pants pocket, climbed the last step, and made my way back to the party. The front door was only 35 feet away from me. I picked up my pace and . . .

"Colin! There you are, Colin Greene! I've got Clarence right here!"

I froze in my steps. My shoulders were practically in my ears. I felt the stolen Bully Book page burning a hole in my pocket, giving off a glow anyone could see.

"Clarence, this is Colin Greene. He's been doing our walks."

I turned slowly, like a snake charmed by Ms. Corbinder's

voice. And there he was: tall, dark hair flowing down over his eyes. Dark eyes, like he was wearing a bit of makeup, like a goth kid. Strange.

"Are you Richard Greene's little brother?" he said flatly, a combination of suspicion and boredom. "You don't look like him."

"Well . . . I'm glad about that," I said, trying to seem natural.

Clarence gave a small laugh. "That is something to be glad about." His face turned serious. "But why are you here? I don't know you."

Ms. Corbinder nudged him lightly on the arm. "Clarence, Colin does our walks, I told you. You be nice."

"I'm being nice, right?" Clarence said. His look seemed to pierce my lie. He knew that I had The Bully Book page, I could sense it. He knew my name wasn't Colin Greene. There was silence and staring for what felt like a minute.

"Well, I need to attend to our guests." Ms. Corbinder broke the stalemate. "You two play nice."

She left, but Clarence never looked away. "Really. What are you doing here?" he repeated.

"Just like your mom told you." I swallowed my fear. "I do your walks . . . I like birthday parties."

Clarence leaned in close and examined my face like he was checking my pores for dirt. I was extremely tense. For a moment, I was sure he had caught me.

But then he pulled back, and his expression turned to boredom again. He left me without a word and disappeared behind the elbows and hairdos of the people at the party.

I made my way out the door and biked home—ecstatic. Like I'd escaped from the cave of a dragon.

I have a Bully Book page. It's in my hands right now.

After Me

I hope you understand what I'm saying.

I wish I could just talk to you. I would tell you these things and I would check on you. But I can't do that. This book will stay here at the school, but I'm moving on to bigger things.

I just want people to know what I did here this year. I don't want to be forgotten.

But I also know I can't be connected to this. I'm going to be an important person someday, a lawyer or politician—maybe the president. And I'll get there using the lessons in this book.

But if anyone finds out I wrote it, my career could be ruined.

So just like you've got to keep this book secret, I have to guard my identity. And I just hope the book can live on its own.

You have to keep it going.

Journal #29

I don't have a clue what to do with this thing.

How to Make Trouble without
Getting in Trouble, Rule the School,
and Be the Man

I guess it's pretty self-explanatory, but this page really only says that it's a book that will teach you how to be cool. After that, there's nothing. There isn't a single thing about how to pick the Grunt.

How can I change my fate from reading a single page?

At least it proves the conspiracy is real. That's saying something. But I already see the evidence everywhere.

I was doing my recess routine today, walking around with my hands in my pockets, mumbling to myself: general loser stuff. I could see Adrian and Jason had started a game of football and all the guys were pushing each other around. Melody was playing four-square with Ruth.

Then I saw something strange. Colin and Donovan were

off together, in the field past the jungle gym. Donovan was stalking around Colin in a circle. Colin stood frozen.

As I walked toward them, I could hear what Donovan was saying.

"You're the grossest, Colin. You're a slimeball. You're wet like you just came out of your mom. Do you still kiss your mom, Colin? Are you that gay?"

"Hey!" I said, not thinking. "Why don't you shut up, Donovan?"

A strange feeling came over me. I didn't know why I said it, and even though I knew it could be trouble, I wasn't sorry and I wasn't scared.

Donovan's shirt came untucked and he pulled it back down over his stomach. The pudge was returning.

"What did you say?"

I was surprised by it myself. I faced around to Colin, who seemed terrified, and realized how wrong this all was. Here in the field, it was just me, Colin, and Donovan. A few years ago, we might have been just hanging out together. But now there was this ridiculous Book in charge of everyone.

I hate The Bully Book and I hate the Grunt.

"Stop making fun of Colin. It makes you sound like an idiot. And stop calling people gay. I don't even know why that's an insult. There are real gay people in the world, you know, and there's nothing wrong with them. Calling someone gay, like it's a bad thing, is like calling someone a dentist—it doesn't make any freaking sense!"

It felt good to chew Donovan out. He's been playing a part all year. He's not an evil mastermind, he's just Donovan White: the kid who ate markers in art class.

But obviously, Donovan hadn't thought about this stuff like I had. He's more of an action man. And pretty quickly, I was on the ground.

All I saw was a fuzzy peach color coming at my face. But it was no peach, I'll tell you that. Donovan's head slammed right into my nose and knocked me to the ground.

He had me pinned with his elbows against my shoulders. I could hear the cavalry, Jason and Adrian, making their way over. In the second before they got there, Donovan leaned real low down and he whispered raspy in my ear.

"Eric. We were friends. But you're the Grunt now. I'm cool and you're not. You can't talk to me, and you can't touch me."

Then Jason and Adrian showed up. Jason, of course, started screaming swear words at me, calling me every name he could think of. He said if I told on Donovan to Principal Clark, he and Adrian would say that Donovan acted in self-defense—that I attacked him. And since I was the one with the record of getting in fights—he looked at Colin—no one would believe anything I said.

That's the thing about Jason. He's no idiot. And when Melody's not around, he does whatever he wants.

"You better be watching your back, Grunt," he said, leading The Evil Three away with the rest of the kids. "'Cause if you keep stepping like this, we're gonna get ya. I'm serious." He karate-kicked the air, and for once I was truly scared by it. I'd always thought Jason's moves were just lame showing off, but after actually getting hit by someone, I could imagine what that foot could do to my face.

Once they'd all left, Colin picked me up. "You think they'll really come get you?" he said, not even thanking me.

"I don't know."

Things were changing all right, but not for the better. I reached up to my nose and felt the wetness. Blood. Not a big deal, I thought, I can suck it up.

I left Colin in the field and snuck into the school. I didn't want any hall monitors or whatever to see my bloody face. I'd just get in more trouble. I assessed the damage in the bathroom.

My nose and lips were all covered with blood, but my shirt was thankfully clean. I took paper towels and wiped away what I could, but it kept dripping down. I ran the faucet and tried to wash it off. And that worked a little better. I put pressure on it to try and stop the bleeding.

I checked the mirror to see if anything showed. There were no traces of the fight. But I was shaking.

Like a leaf.

Paint a Pretty Picture

You're going to be messing with the Grunt pretty bad. And I'm telling you, one day it will all blow up in your face. Unless you're careful.

Make the Grunt look bad to your teachers, to the recess monitor, to the principal. Take the time when things are calm and make little complaints about the Grunt. Don't wait until the Grunt's gotten you in trouble. Mention that he was swearing at recess, playing too rough at football, asking to copy other kids' assignments.

Nothing that will get the Grunt called to the office. Just make it so teachers don't really trust him.

And then, one day, when the Grunt tries to get you in trouble and you have to tell a story to get yourself out of it, it will be much easier because nobody will trust him over you.

You've only been accused once, and you have friends to back you up. The Grunt has a million little black marks on his record.

That's being prepared.

Journal #30

What they never show in the movies is that a punch in the nose means picking out bloody boogers for a week.

It's disgusting, I know. But you've got to get them or they clog up and turn you into a mouth breather.

Blood boogers every twenty minutes is not helping my sanity. It's like a reminder of what Jason said. "We're gonna get you."

I feel watched. When I'm dropped off at school in the morning to when I'm walking home from the bus stop. I feel eyes on me.

Yesterday, I was leaving school kind of late. It's warmer now and I've been riding my bike home; I thought I heard someone behind me. I turned around, but the parking lot was deserted.

There was a big crash as I rounded the corner of the school. I caught a glimpse of someone running away from the bike racks. My bike was tipped over and tangled with a few others.

I didn't see who did it.

Melody came up to me in school today. I feel like we've

been avoiding each other the last couple months. I'm definitely avoiding her. I wonder if she knows her boyfriend is making threats on my life, or that I got head butted in the nose last week.

"What's up, Eric?" she said. She talks to me in this real bright voice, like how you talk to a little kid or a dog. We're reading about nonverbal communication in science class. One kind of nonverbal communication is tone of voice. But I can't figure out what she's trying to say.

It makes me nervous to talk to anyone nowadays. I don't like thinking that they can know what I'm feeling from the tone of my voice, or my body language. That stuff's too hard to control.

I'm afraid that if I even say "Hi" to Melody, she'll know everything that's going on inside of me.

Because the things going on inside are not pretty.

So I didn't say anything to her at all. But as I was walking away she said, in a weird tone of voice:

"Eric. Are you mad at me?"

*****

You have no idea.

What People Want

If you think shy people don't want to be noticed, you're wrong. They just want to be seen in their own way.

Everybody wants to be seen in their own way. That's why they choose the clothes they do, talk how they do, and lie how they do. Everybody is acting the way they want you to see them.

Guys that throw up gang signs want you to think they're tough. Girls that wear tons of makeup want you to think they're confident. But, of course, real tough guys don't need to show it and confident girls don't have to cover themselves.

Shy people aren't dumb. They know how easy it is to see through that kind of stuff. They don't want you to see through them, so they disappear.

Figure out how the kids in your class want to be seen. Then treat them that way. Even though you know it's a front.

They'll be grateful.

Journal #31

Not getting too far in interpreting the Bully Book page, so I thought I'd go a different way. I went back to the library and pulled the 6th-grade yearbooks for all known Grunts: Richard, Daniel, and myself.

I wrote out all the things I knew about us, trying to find what we had in common. I ended up with a big, messy list. It went nowhere.

The last thing I remember, I was writing down everything I knew about the Grunts' eating habits—and then I must have fallen asleep.

Next thing I knew, the library windows had gone dark. I was groggy and the corner of the table was imprinted on my forearm. I checked my digital watch: 7:34 p.m.

No.

Mom would not be happy about this.

I threw the yearbooks back on the shelf and left the library. The school was dark and deserted. But luckily the doors weren't locked from the inside.

The streetlamps were on in the parking lot. They made

two big pools of yellow light on the snow and pavement. The bike racks were under the lamp on the Old Side of the school. Even way over from the New Side entrance, I could see my bike was the only one left on the rack.

It was so cold it hurt. My hands were like flippers and I could barely fish the bike key out of my jeans. I put it between my teeth and tried to adjust my gloves. Then I saw something that made my mouth drop open, and the key fell in the snow.

My bike had a chain wrapped around it. Not my U lock. A thick black chain. A heavy padlock kept it fastened tight.

Someone's stalking me, I thought. They tied up my bike so I couldn't escape, and now they're behind me, getting ready to attack. I felt around for the key but didn't dare to look down. My ears were pressed to the night.

Snow crunched under a boot.

I forgot the key and ran. I had no destination, just away from the trap. I heard a voice behind me. I ran faster.

This is what Jason had threatened. They were coming to get me. I shouldn't have talked back to Donovan. Mom always said, "Even if you don't agree with the laws, even if you think they're crazy, you follow them or you get into trouble." She was right. I could think The Bully Book was as dumb as I liked, but I'm living in their world now. They make the rules.

I charged over Evergreen Road and knew I couldn't keep this pace. Every recess, while I'm walking around with my hands in my pockets, these guys are playing football. I could hear their voices behind me. I ran into the woods.

If I could make it to the bottom of the ravine, I thought I could lose them. I'd been in this chase before, with Daniel. If I watched my step, I could make it.

Behind me, I heard a thump and a yell. Maybe they fell, I thought. I hoped so, because it was pitch-black out here and we'd gone at least a quarter mile from all humanity. It was cold and quiet and no one could hear when I screamed.

And I did scream. The snow in the ravine wasn't crispy like in the parking lot. Underneath the pristine whiteness was a layer of deadly ice. One moment, I was speeding down a hill, and the next, I was on my back, staring up at the stars.

My legs felt numb and sore at the same time. I think a tree root was wrapped around my foot, because I couldn't move.

My backpack was strapped beneath me and the textbooks stabbed my shoulder blades. Snow crunched under a boot. I tried to flip myself to my stomach but my arms were weak. A tree branch snapped under a hand. I pulled at my foot to free it, but couldn't get the right angle and it was too hard to lift my head. The moon was above my face. Safe and far out in the sky. A dark shadow came across it.

"You have something of mine," said a voice. I winced, I couldn't even lift my arms to protect myself. I got ready for the punch.

"You have something of mine and I want it back." The voice said again. Had what? I thought. I didn't take anything from them. The figure leaned low over me and the moonlight off the snow lit up his face. A dark eye blinked blankly.

"Clarence!" I gasped, and coughed uncontrollably. The fall had knocked the wind out of me. I was up against the wrath of a psychopath. I coughed and coughed.

He grabbed me by the straps of my backpack, kicked the tree root pinning my leg, and pulled me up to my feet. He was surprisingly strong. He looked down at me with black eyes. The night reflected in them like angry stars.

"Do you have what you took from me?" he asked slowly and, I could tell, for the last time.

"Uh . . ." My mind struggled to work. Everything was falling apart. I had the page but didn't know what to do with it. Now I was going to lose it, and God knows what else. "Yeah," I said, "in here."

Clarence pushed me aside and ripped off my backpack like an animal. He yanked it open in a panic. I caught my breath while he emptied it, every book, every paper. They all went into the snow until he got what he wanted—the laminated page. The Bully Book. He held it up to the moonlight, and in its glow, I saw a look of relief on his face.

In an instant, the laminated page was tucked away in Clarence's own bag. He refilled my backpack and handed it over.

"Are you going to be all right getting home?" he asked, all trace of emotion gone.

"Yeah, I think so," I said, unsure of myself. How much trouble was I in with this guy? What was he going to do to me?

"Sorry for locking your bike. I had to keep you here somehow."

"Well, it worked . . . " I said nervously.

"The combination to the padlock is just 1-2-3-4. Keep it if you want, or throw it away. I don't care." Clarence turned away from me and started walking up the side of the hill. I couldn't believe it. That was all he was going to do? Not beat me up, not anything?

"Eric," he said, turning around. "You and I have a lot in common. More than you know. Come by my house this Saturday. I imagine you know . . . how to get in."

Standing on My Shoulders

Nobody helped me with any of this. I want you to remember that. My life has not been easy.

There was nobody giving me a handbook of what to do. I had to make it up for myself. Something you'll never experience.

This year, we did American history in social studies class. We learned all about Benjamin Franklin and John Adams and Thomas Jefferson. The men who wrote the Declaration of Independence and the Constitution and started the Revolutionary War. A kid in my class, a real idiot, interrupted the teacher. He asked her, "Why do we need to learn about these old, dead guys?" Everyone in the class started laughing. I got so mad.

"Because," I said to this idiot. I stood up and shouted real loud. "Because," I said, "they invented the entire country you're living in. They made it up. You can just sit back because they spent their entire lives making a country that'll last ten thousand years. You better know their names."

Everybody got real quiet after that one.

You gotta give respect to the people that came before you and set things up. The Founding Fathers worked hard on America. They struggled their whole lives so we could sit around and enjoy it.

It's always that way with people who make great things. Everybody that comes after really gets the benefits.

Journal #32

"I don't believe it!"

Clarence looked strange laughing, but he was doing it anyway. We were in the depths of his basement, which wasn't as scary with the lights on.

"Thought I was a Bully Booker, oh my God!" Clarence kept it up, doubled over laughing.

I had come over first thing Saturday morning, not knowing why Clarence wanted to see me again.

"You thought that"—Clarence pushed the hair from his eye—"when we were on the same mission all along."

Clarence isn't the author of The Bully Book. That's not to say he has nothing to do with it. Clarence is the 10th-grade Grunt.

I should have known when I saw his picture in the yearbook. He has the same sad expression as Richard and Daniel. His goth-kid tendencies would naturally keep him from being too popular. And at his birthday party, there were no kids. I thought they might have been upstairs.

"That's where we put the coats," Clarence told me.

Clarence's story wasn't too much different from my own, just more extreme. Things turned bad in 6th grade, and being an intelligent kid, Clarence wondered why. He'd heard rumors about a conspiracy, a sort of secret organization, but it wasn't until he dropped his pen in a school trash can that he found proof. Along with his pen, Clarence pulled up a note that mentioned himself and his three worst bullies.

"This was the start of my collection." Clarence flung open the double doors of his enormous file cabinet and picked a crumpled sheet of paper from a left-hand drawer.

Keepers of The Book—
Tonight we'll meet again in the dark part of the parking lot. Clarence is doing well as the Grunt, but we still need to study The Book and strategize. Neil Armand is forming a base of power separate from ours. We need to take him down.

Finding that note set Clarence on an insane quest. Desperate to figure out his situation, he began combing every trash can in the school at the end of the day. He's kept this up for the past 4 years. Even after leaving elementary school, he would make it his business to find that year's Bully Bookers and gather what information he could on them. He would come to the elementary school secretly, after hours, and pick through the tests, essays, and notes the students had thrown away. He brought all of his findings here, to his basement lair, where he organized and analyzed each day's find.

"Most of it's junk," he said to me, flipping through the collection. "But every so often, you find something worthwhile."

He handed me a disciplinary report he'd found when the office dumped out all their old files:

ARBORLAND SCHOOL DISTRICT

1300 Gedes Avenue
Arborland, MI 48104

From the desk of Arthur J. Weiss
Arborland Elementary School
Principal

Student: Kevin Bushwald
Age: 11
Height: 4'10"

Kevin was suspended for attacking two other boys. The boys claim that Kevin approached them while playing a basketball game. Kevin took the ball from them and when the boys asked for it back, he lunged at them, punching them repeatedly in the chest. Several children at the scene corroborated the boys' story.

Kevin, however, claims that the boys attacked him and the entire class is part of a conspiracy. He further claims the boys possess a book that advises them on ways to torment Kevin and control the class. I am recommending Kevin for psychological counseling.

—Counselor, David Britman

"That's a ten-year-old report," Clarence said, smiling. "I've been trying to contact Kevin Bushwald since I got it, but all I know is that he moved out of the state."

"Ten years old?" I said. "He and his Bully Bookers are in college by now. I didn't know how far back this goes."

"No one knows. Can't believe you thought I started it."

"You freaked Daniel out pretty bad."

"I know," Clarence said seriously. "But it was for his own good."

Clarence had discovered that Daniel's Bully Bookers were using a particular tree house to conduct their meetings. Brilliantly, he snuck in one night and hid a baby monitor in the corner so he could listen in. Like me, he wanted to know why he'd been picked to be the Grunt, and what he could do about it.

On the day Daniel tore out the page of The Bully Book, Matt Galvin called an emergency meeting of his own Evil Three. Clarence heard the Bully Bookers' plan to ambush Daniel the next morning and retake the page.

Out of concern for a fellow Grunt, but also drooling at the possibility of having a page of The Bully Book, he surprised Daniel as he came home that night, and intimidated him into giving up the page.

Thinking ahead, Clarence photocopied and laminated the page for himself. He then took the original to Matt Galvin's house and slid it through the crack of his bedroom window. He had placed it in an envelope with a note:

I've picked up your slack. No one else is to find out about this.
Signed, a disappointed Keeper of The Book.

Clarence's message probably saved Daniel from getting the beating of his life. The Bully Bookers must have gotten suspicious of being spied on by older Bully Bookers, because the baby monitor no longer picked up a signal and they moved their meetings to another location Clarence couldn't find. He still had the page, though like me, Clarence couldn't make any sense of it. Nothing explaining why he was chosen for the Grunt. All it did was confirm and remind him of his fate.

"I'd like you to join with me, Eric," Clarence said, his long story over. "You've gotten this far. I think we could help each other."

"What do you mean?" I asked.

"I'm saying we should combine forces, share information. I promise you, The Bully Book keeps its claws on you well past 6th grade. I still have a stake in this. You can help me, and I, you." He gestured to his enormous filing cabinet. "I want you to read the archives. I've been through them a hundred times already. I need fresh eyes. Maybe you'll find something I've missed. Maybe together we can finally take this home."

"Take it home. You mean find The Bully Book?"

"What else is there?" he said. Clarence offered his hand to me. "Shake on it?"

"Shake on it."

I slid open a drawer, pulled out a stack of papers, and got to work.

Didn't Hear It Coming

If a tree falls in the forest and nobody's there to hear it, does it make a sound?

Of course it makes a sound, but the point of this old saying is: If no one can hear it, what does it matter?

I don't really like this saying, because besides trees falling down, there's other stuff happening in the world that you can't see or hear. Stuff you probably care about.

Maybe somewhere right now your parents are talking about how you're doing bad in school and they're going to ban you from watching TV. Maybe right now one of your lieutenants is off somewhere making fun of you. He's laughing at the way you walk or talk or eat your Jell-O, and from now on, every time you do one of those things, he and God-knows-who-else are going to be smirking inside.

Laughing at you, and you won't even know it.

I think this is happening all the time. People are talking about you behind your back, you're doing weird things in their dreams, you're in the background of strangers' vacation photos and hanging up on the walls of their house.

That's why I make all my lieutenants report to me whenever they hear my name mentioned. It's why I make sure I'm friends with the most gossipy kids in class. I need to know what people think about me in my kingdom.

The scariest thing about the world is knowing it goes on when you're not there.

If a tree falls in the woods, I want to hear it come down.

Journal #33

The variety of stuff you can find in Clarence's archive is extraordinary. I've been working my way through several categories of papers at once, just to keep things interesting.

I found a letter from an old principal detailing all the improvements that have been made to the school since the 60s. It turns out we didn't get hand driers in the bathrooms until 2004.

There are personal papers too. Piles and piles of love letters, notes, after-school plans, IOUs, and cheat sheets. These have been my favorite to read, and Clarence says they're the most likely to contain clues. We know the Bully Bookers write notes to each other discussing their meetings, because we have one.

Or Clarence has one. Sometimes I feel like it's my collection too.

I work alone lately. Clarence says he's read everything in here and has a good memory for it. He says I've got fresh eyes, maybe I can find something he missed. He'll come down and check on me every once in awhile. Maybe bring something to eat.

I've been over here every day for a couple of weeks now, so it's turned into a ritual. Clarence spends the early afternoons over at the elementary school fishing through the trash cans. He gets home around 4 and comes downstairs to read what he found and drop it in the archives.

He'll heat up a frozen dinner and say, "Anything, Eric?"

If I've got something to show him, I'll hand it over. But it's rare that I have anything really good. So I say, "Nothing, Clarence."

Nothing.

But today I found something . . . strange.

Melody M—

What's up girl! This is so boring! Why do we need to learn about stuff that happened a million years ago? Ahh!

Here is a quiz that I have created especially for you.

FILL IT OUT AND GIVE IT BACK TO ME AS SOON AS POSSIBLE OR I WILL DIE OF BOREDOM!!!

1. What do you want to be when you grow up?

   A veterinarian because then I can spend time with dogs all day and make them feel better when they're sick.

2. What will your husband look like?

   Oh my God, I have no idea! I don't even know if I'll get married. You need to go to school for a long time to be a veterinarian.

3. *What is your dream house?*

My dream house is a place on Lake Michigan where I can have a sailboat and a canoe.

4. *Who is your best friend?*

Duh! You!

5. *Who is your worst enemy?*

I don't have a worst enemy, but there is someone who gets on my nerves. You know who I'm talking about.

6. *Who do you like? (sworn to secrecy)*

You always ask me this! I don't know if I "like" anybody. But Eric Haskins is really nice. He's super funny and we always talk to each other at recess and our moms are friends.

7. *How am I supposed to survive this class?*

By writing me another quiz :)

My hands were sweating. Clarence took a plate of lasagna out of the microwave. He put it down in front of me.

"Anything, Eric?"

I looked up at him. Did he see the quiver in my lip? Could he hear the thumping in my chest?

"Nothing, Clarence."

He sighed and sat down at his desk. He started reading that day's haul. My eyes went back to the note.

Is Melody M who I think she is? This must be her. My name is spelled out in black and white. Melody Miller is the only Melody I know.

It's not like she comes right out and says she likes me. But under the question "Who do you like?" she wrote my name. Reading this you could interpret it as: If I had to say I liked someone, it'd be Eric Haskins.

Maybe that's going too far. But maybe not. It is my name there. In curly, girly handwriting.

"Clarence," I said, trying to act casual. "When were these notes found? In this section here." I gestured to the part of the drawer I took Melody M's note from.

"Um, those . . ." Clarence put a finger to his lip. "Last year. Yeah, that whole section is from late last year. Why?"

"No reason," I said. Clarence went back to his reading

and I went back to mine.

Eric Haskins is really nice. Nice. Like a nice car. Or a nice shot in a basketball game.

He's super funny. Funny. Like a lovable guy you just always want to be around.

We always talk to each other at recess. Always. She can't get enough of me.

Our moms are friends. Moms. We both have moms and they know each other.

Oh my God. Melody likes me. And she likes me enough to tell her best friend about it, even though I'm not sure who that refers to. Melody had about 5 best friends last year.

But she likes me.

Maybe she was okay mentioning it to a friend in a private note, but when that whole Facebook thing happened it was just too public for her. Dating can be a scary idea. You shouldn't just drop it on someone where everybody can see. I should have talked to her about it afterward. I should have told her it was a prank, and that she was still my friend. Instead I avoided her, and that made it look like the Relationship Request was real and I was just embarrassed by it.

I hate to say this, but I think Jason did it the right way.

He talked to her about going out in private, over a weekend. They figured it out by themselves before they went public.

I still have trouble believing it's real, though. It always seemed like she hated Jason, and she obviously knows how mean he is. I feel like she's just dating him because he's popular.

She didn't write Jason Crazypants's name, did she? No. She wrote Eric Haskins. She wrote me.

I need to figure this out.

Journal #34

I asked Melody to be my math partner. Just on a little worksheet, no big deal, but still, I stepped right in front of Jason Crazypants, blew right by him, and said, "Melody, do you want to be my partner?"

Jason was standing right there, but Melody didn't pay him any attention. She smiled, big and white. "Sounds great!"

We worked though the story problems together, and, at first, I tried not to joke around or act like everything was okay. But there were these kids in the story problems, Joe and David and Karen, and they were endlessly trying to divide up jars of jellybeans and mow lawns at different angles and measure the heights of flagpoles. Melody turned to me and said, "If Eric and Melody have 15 story problems left between them, and they each take 2½ minutes to solve, but Melody can only take another half hour of this before going insane, how many problems will Eric and Melody solve before her brain explodes?"

I laughed, and she laughed, and then we were like that

for the rest of the day, making jokes, not talking about anything serious. After school, we were waiting for her mom to come get us. That's when she brought it all up again.

"Eric, we're okay now, right?" she said.

"What do you mean?"

"Like . . ." She hesitated. "Are you still mad at me?"

I looked away from her.

"Mad about what?"

"I don't know. For whatever was wrong this year." She touched my arm. "You've been avoiding me."

"You were avoiding me!"

"I tried talking to you," she said. "You just ignored me."

"Well . . ." I took a breath. "It makes it kind of hard for us to be friends when you're dating him."

Melody crossed her arms.

"I know that you don't like Jason," she said, "but he's getting better."

"He's evil."

"I'm trying to make him better. That's one of the reasons I said I'd go out with him."

"Oh, great reason!" I said.

"I tried to make things better for you, too."

"Well, it hasn't worked!"

For a minute I thought about telling her everything—the whole year, everything I'd learned about The Bully Book. I'd let her know that everything Jason had been saying to her was lies—that I was the only one who really knew what was happening in this grade. I was going to trust her, and that was a big deal. If she told Jason I knew about The Book, my investigation would be over. The Bully Bookers would block my path every way they knew how and make my life even more horrific. But I decided I'd trust her, because we had been such good friends. I was going to put it all out on the line—and then he showed up.

"Why don't you step away from my girlfriend, gaywad?"

Jason Crazypants is so articulate.

He was behind me with Adrian and Donovan at my sides, boxing me in.

"Jason, cut it out," Melody said quietly. So quietly Jason pretended not to hear.

"She doesn't like you, Grunt." The other kids at the lot turned to look at us.

"What do you think, Haskins?" Adrian said. "You think you're cool?"

"You're gay," Donovan said to me without emotion. The Book has changed him completely.

"He's the Grunt! He's gay! We're gonna make him pay!" Jason Crazypants started chanting. He stepped between Melody and me. "He's the Grunt! He's gay! We're gonna make him pay!"

He was leaning into me, burning anger on his face. Adrian and Donovan joined in on the chant. They had encircled me. I was backing away from them. Other kids at the bus stop started, too.

"He's the Grunt! He's gay! We're gonna make him pay!"

Kids in our grade, but younger ones as well, kids that don't even know me. Why do they hate me when they don't even know me?

It's all a fraud. These Bully Bookers are playing everyone, manipulating them into doing their bidding.

I want to say, "Yes, bow to your masters! You've all been tricked!" But the words won't come out of my throat. My whole brain is flooded with Jason's hateful face, chanting at me. Adrian, Donovan, every kid at this stop.

All except Melody. She's in the back, behind the mob. And it looks like she's shouting too. "Stop it!" I could read it on her lips. "Shut up!"

But the mob was too loud and too thick. She couldn't be heard or break through them. She was in too deep, and when her eyes met mine, I could see that they were full of tears. But she didn't stay to defend me. She ran away and I couldn't blame her. There's nothing that she can do, and pulling her into this would just make life worse for everybody.

So I ran too.

But in the opposite direction.

Journal #35

It's lunchtime. I had to pee. Normal, right?

No, not normal. 'Cause when I got up out of my seat and headed to the cafeteria exit, The Evil Three all dropped their lunches and stood. Maybe they needed to pee too?

Seemed like it, 'cause they were following me. Not even trying to conceal it. I could hear their sneakers on the linoleum flooring. I looked over my shoulder and they were smiling at me, all three of them moving real slow.

I could tell they were trying to scare me. But I didn't let them. I kept walking.

I slipped into the bathroom without looking back. I didn't care what they were doing and I wanted them to know it. I got in front of a urinal and did my private thing. A footstep echoed against the tiles and then Jason and Adrian were on both sides of me. Maybe Donovan was guarding the door.

I think they were pretending to pee, but of course, I didn't look. If they were gonna mess with me again and try to get me to pee myself, they were fools, 'cause I wasn't falling for it.

It took a long time to finish and they just stood there, silent. Adrian had his big sports goggles up on his forehead, which made him cross-eyed a little. Jason was breathing hard, letting out little sighs.

I finished up, zipped myself, and stepped away from the wall. Just then the two of them turned on me. I knew they weren't really peeing. Adrian gave me a cross-eyed look and put his left hand on my shoulder. I didn't really see his right hand, but I felt it.

In my stomach. The fist lingered there for a second. I bent over and coughed. His big arm pulled away and another hand was on my neck, pulling me up from behind. Again. The thin fist this time. It was Jason and it didn't hurt as much, cause my stomach was all tensed up now. He grabbed my shirt collar and pulled my head up to his mouth.

"Mind your place, Grunt." He pushed me away.

I didn't get a good view of them leaving. But I think they did it real slow.

Getting Your Hands Dirty

Now, I know I've talked about physical violence, and I've told you not to do it. Generally, this is true. It's a very risky thing to hit a kid. It doesn't fit the image we're going for. So if you have to do it, absolutely no one can know.

My dad talks about a thing called "Risk/Reward." It's where you weigh all the bad things that can happen from doing something against all the good things. On the risk side, you can get in trouble, kids might think you're a jerk, and you could get into a real fight and be hurt.

There aren't too many rewards. The only one is controlling your Grunt. And if it comes to that, it's worth it.

An out-of-control Grunt is one who talks back to you or your lieutenants. A Grunt who doesn't do what you say. Or even one who is not obviously scared of you. You need to take quick action, and physical violence might be what you have to do. If you've done your job giving the Grunt a bad reputation with teachers, he won't tell on you.

Leave no marks. They speak, too.

Journal #36

Every day for the last two weeks, when I tried to get up during lunch to use the bathroom, Jason and Adrian would stare me down. I've been trying to hold it until the end of school.

But the science experiment I've been running on my bladder went wrong today when my mom again packed 2 Hi-Cs for lunch.

I had to get to the bathroom.

I heard chairs screeching away from the lunch table. The Evil Three were after me again.

But I had a plan.

Which was to run. But not just anywhere. I was heading to the side of the school where nobody uses the bathrooms, not even the janitors. I ran to the Old Side.

Down the long hall I went. The bright red bricks of the New Side flashed past until I hit the plaque that marked the Old Side. From here on out, the school is built of white concrete blocks.

Nobody likes these bathrooms. The sinks are all broken

and spray a permanent mist into the air. It's like walking through a jungle. The mirror is cracked and if you flush the urinals, they flood the floor with 5 gallons of water and pee. It stinks, and it's wet, and The Evil Three would never find me there.

I was just relaxing when the handle of the urinal squirted me in the face.

God, I thought, wiping the water away with my hand, the Old Side is so old.

And that's when it hit me. All the nice stuff is on the New Side of the school, while the crappy stuff the little kids use is on the Old Side. And there's a reason for that: The Old Side is what the school was originally. The New Side was built later.

My hands were shaking. I did my best to wash them in the mist from the sink, but just ended up soaking my shirt. It didn't matter.

I bolted from the bathroom and down the hall. My sneakers were wet from the bathroom floor, but instead of slipping, I glided down the hallway. Faster than I've ever moved. The concrete blocks shot past. Their white painted patterns guided me to my goal. I hit the brakes and squeaked to a stop.

Right in front of the plaque that marks the end of the Old Side, and the beginning of the New.

In the summer of 1987, Arborland Elementary School was expanded. Under the supervision of Superintendent Irving Davis, a new wing was added, providing modern classrooms and an administrative center. These welcome additions were made possible by a generous gift from the family of Ronald and Harriet Stullman.

I need to get out of school.

Now.

I need to call Clarence.

Looking out the Window

The older I get, the stranger the world seems. Maybe I just understand it better. Every time you put the TV on, there's something happening in some country you never heard of. Last night I saw a TV movie about a nuclear bomb hitting us. It started out really boring and I wanted to leave, but my dad said it was important to see how dangerous things are.

The movie got good after the nuke went off. People's houses were gone and cities were destroyed and everybody was sick and starving and trying to understand what happened. My mom cried during this part where a baby dies. At the end, they kept saying the survivors had to band together and make a new society from the rubble. After the movie, they played a cheesy antinuke commercial.

I wonder what it'd be like if a bomb did go off and destroy everything. I don't want people to die, but when the survivors were talking about building a new society, I got excited.

I've already got a ton of ideas about how to make a better society. We could stop all the wars and things that make life suck.

We could build it from the plan that's in your hands right now.

Journal #37

I found Clarence beginning his daily Dumpster dive.

"We need to get back to the archives. Now."

I jumped on my bike, Clarence did the same, and 5 minutes later I had the 2 documents in my hand. One was a letter written by an old principal of Arborland Elementary and the other was the Bully Book Page itself.

"Look here," I said, and showed Clarence the principal's letter. "Read the thing about 1987."

ARBORLAND SCHOOL DISTRICT

1300 Gedes Avenue
Arborland, MI 48104

From the desk of Arthur J. Weiss
Arborland Elementary School
Principal

Dear Treasurer Shaheen,

In response to your letter, I firmly agree that further improvements to infrastructure need to secure complete funding before they get underway. The incident of the unfinished blacktop has been very embarrassing to the administrative staff as well as unsafe for students. We regret having insufficient funds and appreciate the assistance and generosity of the city treasury. The issue of private funding for a public school is a tough one, and in agreement with your request, I have asked my secretary to research and list all improvements made to the school with private funds. Included below.

1965: Arborland Elementary opens. A parent booster group raises money to purchase a wooden play structure.

1971: New light fixtures are placed in all classrooms. Again, a gift of a parent booster group after complaints of too dim light bulbs.

1983: Energy-efficient windows are installed in all classrooms and hallways to save on heating costs. Funded by a loan from John Pithling, a parent at the school. Loan paid off by 1986.

1987: The Arborland and neighboring Rhetton school districts are in financial crisis. As a cost-saving measure the districts merge. Arborland Elementary is expanded to accommodate the new students and teachers. Expansion is funded by Ronald and

Harriet Stullman, grandparents to a student at the school.

1989: Twenty-eight lockers are added to the locker room to accommodate an expanded athletics program. Again, funding is provided by Ronald and Harriet Stullman.

1997: Five computers are added to the school library. Jointly funded by the city and a parent booster group.

2000: Eight more computers are donated by Miriam Fleishman, a member of the PTA.

2004: Hand driers are added to the bathrooms. Funded by a parent booster group.

And, of course, the blacktop incident in 2007. Private funding is an asset when it's secure, but needs to be handled more rigorously in the future. Thank you again for your support of our school. We welcome your continued questions and oversight.

Sincerely,
Arthur
Arthur Weiss

Clarence's mouth dropped open. I knew he already got it. But I handed him the Bully Book page anyway. "Read the 7th paragraph," I said. Clarence had read it about a million times. He knew it by heart. But he cleared his throat and read out loud:

> "This year, I survived the school district merger, outsmarted kids ten times my size, and completely conquered sixth grade. I've got a ton of friends, everybody does what I say, and teachers don't mess with me. This has been the best year of my life and I made it all by myself."

His mouth just hung open and even the eyeliner couldn't conceal his surprise.

"I don't believe it . . . ," he mumbled.

"You better," I said. "This is the break we needed. I went to the school library after lunch today. The '87 yearbook's not there, so I asked the librarian about it."

"She want to know why?" Clarence said sharply. I could tell he was scared. The trail's been cold so long he got comfortable with his routine. Every day: find papers, file them, go to bed. Now there was detective work to do and real results to be had.

"I told her I was doing a project on the history of the Arborland School District. She said the school doesn't have any yearbooks or student lists before 1998. That's the year they sent everything to the city to be digitized. There's an archive room at City Hall that keeps all the old stuff, but they can't afford a full-time librarian, so the hours are awful."

"When are they open?" Clarence asked me.

"1 p.m. to 3 p.m. on weekdays and 12 p.m. to 2 p.m. on Saturdays."

"So this week's out," Clarence said. "We'll be in school."

"Right." I thought Clarence would suggest we skip school.

"All right, Saturday then," Clarence said, rubbing his hands together. He had a look of unease that I didn't understand. After four years of dedicating his life to this, I'd thought he'd be jumping for joy.

"Do you wanna go get something to eat?" I said. "You know, celebrate or something?"

Clarence looked dazed. "Actually, I've got a lot of work to do today. Homework, you know? So, I can't really . . ."

"Okay," I said, taking a hint. "I guess I'll see you Saturday?"

"Yeah," he said. "For sure." He didn't come up the stairs with me or anything. Just waved good-bye and watched me leave.

I biked home and . . . I guess I've got to sit on this.

Journal #38

I was waiting outside Clarence's house for almost an hour.

I got there at 11:40. Figured we could bike over to City Hall right when it opened. But no one answered the bell. The back door that Clarence was keeping unlocked for me wouldn't open. And there was no response when I knocked on the basement windows.

The lights were all off. No car pulled up in the driveway, no call to my cell phone. Clarence doesn't have a phone of his own, so I just kept calling his house line.

"This is the Corbinder residence. We're not home right now, so please leave a message." Ms. Corbinder's voice on the answering machine.

I didn't leave a message. It was approaching 1 o'clock and I didn't know how much time I'd need.

The bike ride was okay, but I didn't have anyone to talk to. It made me nervous. I kept running scenarios in my head. How the place would be laid out, what I was gonna say.

Inside City Hall, nobody looked at me funny. I guess I'd imagined buff security guards with walkie-talkies guarding the city's center of power. Instead it's a small building filled with bored-looking office workers. Nobody asked me what I was doing there in case I'd make them actually do their jobs. I saw a lot of computer solitaire happening.

I followed the surprisingly informative signs (CITY ARCHIVE ROOM ➲) all the way to the back of the building. A brown door was barely visible in the brown brick wall, but it said CITY ARCHIVE ROOM. I pushed the door open.

Screaming, a silver-haired woman with her bare feet up on a counter nearly kicked herself out of her chair.

I jumped back and closed the door. It was like I'd just walked into the ladies' room or something. I checked the sign on the door again. CITY ARCHIVE ROOM.

"Young man! Young man!" I heard a muffled yell through the door and I opened it a crack. The silver-haired lady had righted herself on the chair and was breathing heavily. She gestured for me to come in. "I'm sorry, young man. I didn't mean to frighten you."

I stepped in a little and looked around the book-lined room.

"You just startled me," she said. "No one usually comes in here. But we are open."

She struggled to put a lacy, gray pair of socks back on as she spoke to me. From the uneven length of her toenails, I could guess she'd been trimming them when I knocked. The clipper on the counter was another clue.

"It's okay," I said. "I'm looking for a yearbook. Arborland Elementary School 1987."

"Right," she said, sweeping toenail shards into the wastebasket. "We can get that found for you." All the books were up on shelves protected by locked glass cases. She jangled some old iron keys and put the appropriate one in the lock. The cabinet opened and, with incredible accuracy for someone who hadn't pulled a book from these shelves in a while, she yanked out the 1987 yearbook and handed it down to me.

The cover was a faded picture of the school with ARBORLAND ELEMENTARY '87 printed in red. The binding was cracked and several pages must have come loose because the whole thing was wrapped around with a rubber band.

"Now, be careful with that, if you please." She gestured to a small desk by the window. "You can read over there, but I'm afraid you can't leave the room with it."

In my hand was the book that could unravel everything and it was barely 30 pages long. Carefully, I removed the rubber band. Page after page, I saw poorly printed photos of the New Side's construction and opening. Dark and grainy photos of kids in their English classes, math, homeroom, music, all the same things we do every day, except everyone in these photos was now grown up.

But one of them left something behind. I got to the page with the 6th graders and realized that somewhere mixed in with these 50 kids was the author of The Bully Book.

Photos took up most of the page, straight on down to the bottom. I searched their names and faces, looking for clues.

They were arranged by order of birthday, and no one struck me as being especially evil.

I figured the only proper way to investigate would be to take down their names and search them on the internet.

I looked at the photos again, hoping something would pop for me, some clue that could make this case easier.

And then I saw it.

Deep in the bottom row, all the way to the right, was a face so pathetic I mistook it for my own. It had the sad-sack look of someone destroyed. The look of Richard, and Daniel, and, come to think of it, Clarence. A Grunt's look.

The name under it was Ronny Whitner. I could not imagine such a sad-looking kid growing up. Much less to be a man who'd come back to the place of his curse, where he'd become a teacher with the sense to spot a fellow Grunt in crisis.

Mr. Whitner, my English teacher.

Journal #39

Saturday, Sunday, Monday, Tuesday rolls around. Still no word from Clarence. I call him, I go to his house. Nothing.

Screw it, I think. I can't sit on this. I'm going solo.

In fact, I'm in Whitner's room right now. Behind the big Reading Board. It's lunchtime and he's in the teacher's lounge. Somewhere, I don't know.

HEY GRUNT is written on the whiteboard in enormous block letters. I put it there. If he isn't the First Grunt, he won't know what it means and he'll just erase it. If he is, I'll see some sort of reaction from him. Recognition. Nothing as extreme as Daniel's, but I'll see it and I'll know.

Then I can move in and get some answers.

There'll be—

Everything in Place

My mom always says, "Set your house in order, that comes first." I think it's from a self-help book, but I never knew what it meant before this year.

When the school districts merged, a lot of new kids came into our sixth-grade class.

And they brought trouble.

Everyone got freaked out about it. Kids that had been friends for years fought over letting new kids into their clique. People got jealous and angry at each other. Sometimes two groups, one from each school, were so similar they had to either combine or fight.

The whole Social Order was turned upside down. The athletic, good-looking kids are at the top. Then you've got the kids who cluster up because they like skateboarding or fashion magazines or volleyball or dance. You've got the weirdos who aren't too popular but float from group to group, keeping the few friends they made in kindergarten. Already this Social Order is unstable, but then double it, with all new people, all new groups, and all new kids trying to prove they're the coolest.

It was a nightmare.

I developed my system out of this craziness to put my house in order, like my mom would say. It took a lot of observation and thought and trial and error, but eventually, I molded my classroom into a nice, well-ordered place, where I was on top and everybody knew it.

It really has been a great year and I couldn't have done it without my Grunt.

Good luck to you, Keepers of The Book.

Journal #40

Whitner walked into the classroom still chewing on a tuna sandwich. I know because I could smell it.

He's a messy eater and not skilled at walking and chewing at the same time. It took all his concentration to keep his chin clean with a napkin and lick all the tuna spread off his fingers. He got to his desk without seeing the whiteboard.

I crunched into a ball. The Reading Board isn't that big. What if Whitner came around behind it and saw me? I should not have placed myself so close to the scene of the crime.

He looked up at the whiteboard and stopped eating his sandwich. I heard an audible smack as his lips separated and the tuna hung lifelessly in his cheeks. It was a long, hard minute before he swallowed.

The sandwich dropped into the trash can. And his open hand curled into a fist. He kicked the trash can so hard it ricocheted against the wall and left his half-eaten sandwich embedded in the bricks. Tuna stink filled the room.

He turned around too quickly for me to see his expression

and stomped out the door. Crap, I thought, he's mad. I crawled my way along the wall and peeked around the doorframe. He was huffing down the hallway to the New Side.

To Clark's office.

I needed to get out of there. My mind flashed back to Clark's behavior assembly. According to the New Rules, harassing a teacher and defacing a classroom are both grounds for a 60-day suspension.

There are just a few weeks of school left. I wouldn't even be eligible for summer school. I'd have to do 6th grade over again. I'd be the Grunt to a whole new group of kids.

I had to know what Whitner was going to do. I took off my shoes and followed him, silently, down the hallway.

He turned the corner down to the administrative offices. I saw him fling open Clark's door. It closed behind him with a swish and then I heard shouting.

Whitner's shouting. It was muffled so I couldn't make anything out but the tone. He was madder than I'd ever heard.

I could see the two of them through the foggy window. Mr. Whitner standing over Clark, his finger in Clark's face.

Clark sitting at his desk, dumbfounded. I put my ear to the glass.

"You childish, ridiculous . . . " shouted Mr. Whitner. Clark said something too soft to hear. "All these years," cried Whitner, "you're the same Tony Clark. My father's dying and you're calling me names! Like we're still in grade school!"

I spun away from the door.

Like we're still in grade school?

I needed to get out of there. Any minute, Whitner was going to open that door and find the vandal hunched over his shoes. I ran back to the cafeteria.

Everyone was eating just like it was a normal day. The world went on for them. They'd go on eating if a meteor was heading toward Earth, just as long as they didn't know about it.

I touched my shirt and it was heavy with sweat. Adrian noticed me first. He tapped Jason on the shoulder and they both started walking toward me. I looked around for somewhere to go. My brain wasn't registering colors and shapes correctly. Everything looked foreign and strange.

The bell rang. Jason and Adrian disappeared.

But I didn't go to class. How could I while the burning thought was on my mind? Music was next. Sometimes Music Lady was bad about attendance.

Forget the consequences. I had to run. I just kept thinking it:

He wasn't in the yearbook. He wasn't there.

On my bike, I checked my watch. 10 minutes into class, and I was halfway to City Hall. It was 12:50 p.m. They'd be opening in 10 minutes. Right on time.

Past the steps of the police station, through the heavy double doors, around the sitting-room chairs and plants, I raced on to the tiny archive room in the back. My steps rang out loudly against the tile floor and even the laziest of the solitaire champions peeked from behind their computers just to see who was this intense young man?

I slammed open the archive-room door with hurricane force and the barefoot silver-haired lady screamed her scream and took the whole desk to the floor level with her.

"I'm sorry," I said, looking down at the heap, "but I need to see the Arborland Elementary yearbook again. 1987."

She was stuck in her fallen chair, so she shot up her hand, the black iron key in her open palm.

I took it and unlocked the correct cabinet from memory. The book was in my lap in seconds and, with a few careful flips, I came to the 6th-grade photo page. Just as I remembered, not a single one of the 50 portraits was a kid-size Principal Clark.

But—I sighed—the portraits ran all the way down the page with no white space underneath.

The pictures did not end on this page.

I lifted the corner of the paper with the index finger of my right hand. I turned the page like someone might turn over a rock concealing a den of hideous cockroaches.

There, in the top left corner of the next page, was the spillover from the 6th-grade photo section. 10 smiling faces that I hadn't seen before.

Especially the photo of a blue-eyed blond boy, his hair perfectly parted, wearing a smile that could conquer the world.

Tony Clark.

Author of The Bully Book.

Journal #41

Clarence is still not picking up the phone. It's been more than 10 days. This is his case, too. But it's like I'm on my own again and it feels awful.

I want him to tell me what to do. No clear road on this.

I have to talk to Principal Clark. That much is obvious. But he's out of my reach. I can't get a handle on him.

I need a way to get him alone. I need to make him talk to me about The Bully Book. He has to tell me how they select the Grunt.

It's the First Grunt who's given me my chance.

Mr. Whitner's been quiet this last week—subdued. Some might say it's because his dad's still sick. He told us his dad has cancer and that's why he's been out of school every Monday. But that's been the situation all year. If you ask me, Whitner's traveled back in time. He thought he'd escaped the Grunt, but you can't get away. It lives in you. All it took was a word on a whiteboard to remind him that he's worthless.

Because classes are over soon, Whitner isn't going to

give us worksheets anymore. We have one final assignment: Interview the Person we Admire Most.

Imagine the pained look in his eyes when I told him who my interview subject would be. Imagine the rage he must have felt when I said I admired the demon of his childhood.

But it's not what you think, Mr. Whitner.

I'm not doing it to make that smiling monster feel special. I'm doing it for people like you and me. I'm doing it for our redemption.

Principal Clark took something from us both.

I'm going to take it back.

Journal #42

"What were you like at my age, Mr. Clark?"

We'd been talking awhile in his office. He said what a surprise it'd been that I chose him for my interview. I told him he'd had an enormous effect on the student population, maybe more than he knew.

"Well," Clark said, straining a little, "I think I was a fairly average kid. Certainly a bigger reader than most. A happy childhood."

"Were you a writer, also?" I said, jotting down some notes.

"A writer? Well . . ." Clark touched the back of his head, as if accessing decades-old memories. "I suppose a little. I hear you're quite the writer, Eric. Mr. Whitner says so."

"Yes, let's talk about you and Mr. Whitner," I said. "I understand the two of you went to school here together."

"That's true. How'd you know that, Eric?"

"Were you friends?"

Clark looked out the foggy office window to the hallway, maybe remembering Mr. Whitner's tirade. "We didn't really run in the same circles."

"Would you say you were . . . enemies?"

"No, Eric. No." Clark adjusted himself in his seat. "And honestly, I don't even know why you'd ask me something like that."

I suppose Bully Bookers don't see Grunts as their enemies, not the way we see them.

"So you never made fun of him, tortured him, humiliated him in class?"

"Eric!" Clark twisted his face in embarrassment. "I don't know where you're . . . Mr. Whitner hasn't been . . ." He looked at me, worried.

"He hasn't said anything to me, Principal Clark." I jotted down more notes. "I'm just asking generally. I'm trying to get a sense of what school was like when you were a kid because, see, at school nowadays, that kind of stuff is fairly common."

Clark picked up a gold pen and rolled it hard between his thumb and forefinger.

"Are you having trouble at school, Eric? Because you know we've got mechanisms to deal with that sort of thing."

"Yes, I'm sure you do. But it's nothing compared to what they have, Principal Clark."

"They? Who is they?"

"You know," I said. My lips were dry, and I wet them. "The ones who have it."

"Have what?" Principal Clark said, leaning closer to me. I could hear the slight grinding of teeth.

I closed my notebook and looked him hard in the eyes.

Who is this man? I thought. The 12-year-old boy who authored The Bully Book? The one who wrecked the lives of my fellow Grunts? Or is he something different now? Grown up and grown out of it.

Mr. Whitner is what happens when Grunts grow up. You never stop being haunted by it. But people like Tony Clark, they change through the years and aren't weighed down by the past. They barely remember it, and the little they do remember—they try to forget.

"There's a legend at our school, Principal Clark." I rose and paced the room. "About a book that will teach you how to rule the class. It's said to be passed down from grade to grade."

Out of the corner of my eye, I could see Clark's hands covering the front of his mouth.

"The Book," I went on, "instructs its Keeper to pick one kid, of specific description, to be the lowest of the low. It calls this one the Grunt." I sat down across from him at his desk. "In your time at our school, Mr. Clark, did such a legend exist? Have you heard about a Book? Have you heard of the Grunt?"

Clark laid his arms across the desk and stared at a mole on his hand. He glanced up at me, his lips pursed in a way I hadn't seen before. I think I found a secret place in him, something he'd never shown the outside world. A private room where he kept his dark secrets. And I was knocking on the door.

"You know, Mr. Whitner's had trouble lately in his classroom." Clark glanced at me sharply. "Heard about it?"

I felt a rising fear in my throat and sat back in my chair.

"No," I said.

Clark nodded, knowingly.

"Because this 'legend' you're talking about, it sounds a lot like some abusive graffiti that was written on his whiteboard."

Like an Olympic wrestler pulling a perfect reversal, Clark had escaped from my chokehold and had me on the mat.

"You know the New Rules. Zero Tolerance. Any student defacing school property receives a 60-day suspension. Plus the 60 days for harassing a teacher."

His tone of voice was completely different. The author of

The Bully Book was showing his face.

"You couldn't even make it up in summer school," he told me.

"But The Book . . ."

"What about it?" He stared at me blankly.

"You covered it up, didn't you?" I felt myself sinking. "How could you not know? How could you forget?"

Clark leaned back in his chair. He considered me, silently.

I might be able to get him fired, but if he nailed me on defacing Whitner's classroom, I was guaranteed to repeat 6th grade. And I wouldn't even get The Book.

I had the most to lose.

"Mrs. Bellemont." Clark buzzed his secretary. "Would you come in and escort Mr. Haskins back to class?"

"Thanks for the interview, Mr. Clark," I said, packing up my stuff. "There sure is a lot about you to admire."

He stood up and grasped my shoulder.

"I try to be good at what I do, Eric." He squeezed my collarbone. "I can't explain it. You know. It's hard . . . when you're a kid."

"Yes, Mr. Clark. It is."

I broke from his grip.

"And you're not making it any easier."

Journal #43

Clarence finally called me.

"Hey, Eric."

"Clarence! Where have you been—I've been calling you all week! I even came to your house!" I said. "Clarence, listen to me, Clarence. I found the author of The Bully Book."

"Yeah . . ." He sighed.

"Yes! It's Tony Clark, Clarence! Principal Tony Clark!"

"Oh."

"What do you mean, 'oh'? This is the biggest news we've ever got!"

"I'm moving, Eric. I didn't want to upset you. My mom and I are moving to Petoskey. High school ended 2 weeks ago, so we've been packing up the house and making trips in the van. Everything's moved now."

I could hear my own breath through the phone.

"We've leaving tonight for good. Sorry I didn't have time to say good-bye. It was all really sudden."

"So you're getting out," I said.

"What do you mean?"

"You're getting out. What do you care? You get a new life."

"Well . . ."

"You're done with it. Moving on. But I can't leave."

I started yelling. "I'm stuck here! This is my world now, Clarence! Get out of it!"

I slammed the phone on the ground.

Clarence kept talking.

"Eric, calm down," the muffled voice said. "You've got to listen to me."

I picked up the cell phone.

"What do you have to say?"

"Listen," he said. "What do you want me to do with the archives? I don't need them now. If you want, I can—"

"I don't want the archives, Clarence. What I want is to be free from this nightmare. Burn them for all I care."

I ended the call.

He's been lying to me. This whole time, he knew. He knew he might escape. Something was wrong when I told him about the plaque. These last weeks while I've been consumed by this, Clarence was planning his escape.

I'm solving a case he started years ago. I get so close and

he doesn't care. He's moving up north to Petoskey.

It's very nice up there. We used to go in the summers when I was a kid.

I'm at a dead end. I still know nothing about The Bully Book and nothing about the Grunt except what it feels like to be him. Next year I'll learn to be a middle-school Grunt.

We can't move, Mom says. She owes more money on the house than it's worth, so she can never sell it. That's what she always says.

I'm tired.

Journal #44

Got our yearbooks today. It was an ice-cream social.

Everybody was going around signing them for each other. I didn't ask anybody, afraid of what they'd write.

Colin wanted to sign my yearbook.

He wrote, "Good knowing you this year, let's still be friends in middle school." It made me wish I'd been nicer to him.

My picture is in there with the other 6th graders'. My hair is slicked and I'm wearing the sweater Mom made me pick, and I've got a purple background. I don't look very happy.

I wondered if some younger kid will be staring at this someday. Some future Grunt looking for answers. I wanted to talk to this kid. I wanted to say to him, "Forget it."

Melody asked to sign my yearbook too.

"Jason and I broke up," she said, taking the book. "He says he wants to be single for middle school."

"Oh." I tried to think of something to say to that.

"It's okay," Melody said. "He was a jerk anyway."

"Sure."

"Well, you knew that, I guess. I really don't know what I was thinking."

I tried not to say something to that.

"What are you doing this summer?" Melody looked up at me. Her eyes were a lighter brown in the sunlight. I don't know when it got so warm.

"Eric?" she said. I looked back at her. "What are you doing this summer? We should hang out."

I tried to write something in her yearbook, but I couldn't put words to this feeling. She was writing furiously in mine.

I handed the yearbook back to her. She gave mine to me.

I closed it without reading the message. She saw that I wrote nothing. Just my initials: E.H.

She frowned a little and stared down her nose.

"Do you think I'm bad?" she asked.

Her freckles are really starting to show. And her skin seems different. She looks older now.

The loudspeaker crackled and gave everyone a shock. Colin spilled ice cream all over his shirt.

"Eric Haskins to the office," it said. "I repeat. Eric Haskins to the office."

It was Clark's voice. Everybody looked at me. Melody asked: "Eric, are you in trouble?"

I picked up my backpack. Stuck the yearbook inside. And looked her straight in the eye.

"Always," I said.

*****

I came into his office and he looked exhausted. Like he hadn't slept in the last three days.

"Have a seat, Eric." He smiled weakly.

"Okay." I sat down.

"Our conversation the other day," he said, his eyebrows bouncing nervously. "Do you remember it?"

"How could I forget?"

Clark frowned at me. "I've been thinking . . . for a very long time. You've reminded me of things."

"Yeah?" I said.

"Yeah." He looked stern. "Things I'd prefer to forget."

Clark stood up, looked at the ceiling above his desk.

"I always thought I understood this school." He was almost talking to himself. "Better than anyone. That's why I went into education, Eric. That's why I came back. You know I could've been anything? Could've been a doctor, a lawyer. I had the grades. Why do you think I made all the New Rules, Eric? Because I wanted this school to be great. I've wanted that since I was 11 years old.

"But sometimes you hurt people," he went on, "when you're trying to do good. And when I do something wrong, I try to make up for it."

"That why you gave Mr. Whitner a job?"

Clark frowned again. "I don't know what he's been telling you, Eric. But I'm trying to do right here. I'm trying to put at rest your fears."

"I'm not afraid of you, Principal Clark. What have you got to say to me?"

"I'm sorry, Eric." He sighed deeply, and sat back down in his chair. "When I was your age, I think I had some problems. At home, in school. I was confused." He rolled his eyes up in his head, searching for the words. "And I did something strange. I made this . . ." He looked at me meaningfully. "I had these gym socks."

"What?" I said.

"I had a pair of gym socks," he said with emphasis. "Terrible ones. I got the idea that I could pass these things down. To the kids in the grade below me, and that they could pass them down, and that could go on for . . ."

"For 25 years," I said.

"So I put the gym socks in my locker. With instructions to pass them down, and directions to keep them there. Locker 337, my favorite number."

"Locker 337," I repeated.

"But," Clark shouted, "I went there this morning. I'd forgotten them years ago. Couldn't believe they'd still be there. I went to the locker, I've got a master list of all th combinations. I opened it up, Eric. This morning."

Clark's eyes widened and he took me by the shoulders.

"It's empty, Eric!" he shouted. "Empty! The socks were lost years ago, there's no truth to that legend, Eric. There's nothing there!"

"Nothing?" I said. My knees weakened and my shoulders slipped out of Clark's grip. I landed in the chair.

"Nothing, Eric!" Clark laughed. He was ecstatic. Like a man freed from death row.

Off the hook in his own mind at least. But I was enraged.

The Book was toying with me. Letting me close and slipping away! My feet shot me up.

"What is the Grunt?" I shouted. "How. Do. You. Pick. The. GRUNT?"

Clark flattened in his chair, shocked.

"Listen to me, Principal Clark. I don't want this life forever!" My voice broke. "Tell me how not to be the Grunt!"

"Eric, I don't know what you're asking."

"You do!" I shouted. "Why won't you tell me?"

Mrs. Bellemont, Clark's secretary, busted in and grabbed my arms. She dragged me across the office, my heels digging into the carpet.

"Bully Bookers forget, Mr. Clark! You grow up!" I shouted. "We live this life forever!"

Clark didn't say another word. He stared at me, like a frightened child. The door to his office swung shut.

Mrs. Bellemont said the only reason I didn't get suspended was that today's the last day and she didn't want to do the paperwork.

Journal #45

Hiding in the bathroom stall right now.

After the confrontation with Clark, I was upset. I went to the locker room to see for myself.

Came here to see the locker. Number 337. Clark left it unlocked. Empty. No Bully Book. Maybe once, but not now.

I was sad. I had gotten so close to solving the mystery. I'm so trapped in my own life. I remembered when Donovan first mentioned The Book, so long ago. Richard's warning. Finding Matt Galvin, meeting Daniel Friedman. The first stolen page. Being so close and so far at the same time. The plaque. Whitner and Clark. The archives. The letter about the construction projects.

I've been carrying my journal around like a casebook. I have every entry on me at all times. Even the one about the 1987 construction. Everything done on the school since the 60s. I'd only looked at one date: The New Side addition. I looked at the letter again, but this time, my eyes fell a quarter of an inch. I saw this:

1989: 28 lockers are added to the locker room to accommodate an expanded athletics program. Again, funding is provided by Ronald and Harriet Stullman.

I noticed that the number 337 on the locker was painted on. Not printed like some of the others. I pulled out a quarter and viciously scratched the number. The twenty-year-old paint cracked easily under my fingers, and revealed an older number below it. 309.

Lockers were added after Tony Clark graduated and some of the numbers had been reassigned. Principal Clark went to the wrong locker this morning!

If 309 became 337, then 337 must have become 365. I slid to 365 and ground the painted number to dust. The true number stared back at me.

In the dim light of the locker room I could peek through the vents of locker 337. I caught a faint whiff of musk, the smell of old papers in my grandfather's damp basement. I caught sight of a few sheets held loosely in a thick leather binder. So ordinary. So close.

I began to hyperventilate, and ducked into the stall to catch my breath.

I don't think I—

Journal #46

This will be my last entry in this journal. Perhaps I will have other journals in my life, but this one has come to an end. I will use what energy I have left to write it properly.

I heard noises when I was in the bathroom stall. And they were just what you'd expect if you had half a brain, but I don't, so I was surprised.

Jason Crazypants, Adrian Noble, and Donovan White came into the locker room together.

"Get The Book," commanded Jason.

"I don't know why we're doing this before school clears out," protested Donovan. "If we just waited an hour . . ."

"I don't want to have to come back here," Jason snarled. "I'm done with this school. I'm never coming back."

"But it's so early," whined Donovan. "What are we gonna do with it until it gets dark?"

"We'll take it up to the old cabin and chill until it's time to start the ceremony," Adrian replied in soothing tones. "Don't worry about it. The ceremony's fun. For us, anyway."

Donovan tried to laugh. "Those 5th graders are in for it!"

"Yeah," Jason laughed. "Bag it. Let's go."

They were taking The Bully Book. It was in the same room with me. Theoretically, I could rush out there and grab it. I could rush out—and get karate chopped by Jason.

I heard them leaving. No time to make a plan. I just followed them . . . quietly.

I tailed them through the Old Side of the school. They were sneaking through the secret back way. I watched them jog off, a red leather binder in Adrian Noble's arms. Outside, I covertly unlocked my bike from the rack.

I kept on them for four blocks, always hanging back a good distance, the sound of their laughter led me on.

Then, there was silence.

I heard nothing. I saw nothing. They had disappeared into Adrian Noble's backyard. They'd said they were going to the old cabin, which is really just this abandoned shack near Lake-in-the-Woods Park. I heard a low buzz and laughter. High-pitched squeals of delight and the sound of a small engine revving up. Then crash! They came bursting out of the bushes in Adrian's backyard, trampling the flowers with a full-size, fully functional golf cart.

I followed the buzzing of the cart and the laughter of

the Bully Bookers all the way up to Lake-in-the-Woods. Over the trail, through the hills. Pumping crazily on my bike. Always out of sight, but within earshot of the cart.

Finally, silence. They stopped and all headed for the cabin at the side of the hills. I hid my bike in some underbrush and slid under the cabin's wooden porch. I lay there for nearly 5 hours.

I heard them joking and laughing and playing music. Then Adrian and Donovan's voices were on the porch, above me.

"Remember when we did this last year?" said Adrian.

"I was scared," Donovan answered.

"Me too, but it worked out real good," Adrian said. "I'm glad the Keepers picked Jason. Or this year would've sucked."

"I'm just glad Jason picked us as lieutenants instead of Grunts!" Donovan laughed.

"Yeah, Haskins did pretty good, didn't he?"

"The Book was right," Donovan agreed. "He was the perfect one."

"Don't you feel stupid!" It sounded like Adrian grabbed Donovan and had him in a headlock.

"Get off me!" yelled Donovan.

"Say it!" Adrian taunted. "Say, 'I was wrong'! Say, 'I'm stupid'!"

"I was wrong!" Donovan gasped. "I'm stupid!"

Adrian laughed. "It's been a good year, bro."

Donovan coughed and I heard them give a weak high five. "Yeah," he said.

"Get in here, fools!" Crazypants yelled from inside the cabin. "There's work to do."

Adrian and Donovan clomped inside.

What were they talking about? I thought. I "did pretty good"? I didn't do anything to help them. They just attacked me. I've been working against them all year.

I wanted to jump out from under the porch and grab them, shake them, and scream, "How did I do good? What did I do good for you?" But I knew that was stupid. They'd overtake me, and here in the woods, I'd have no place to run. The best plan was just to stay calm, lie on the ground beneath the porch, and wait them out. I'd overhear what I could and play the rest by ear.

After a few hours, the sun was setting and Lake-in-the-Woods grew dark. I heard them shoving and razzing each other. I peeked through a crack between two wood planks and watched the three of them board the golf cart, Jason in the driver's seat with Adrian next to him, Donovan standing on the step in the back. Adrian and Jason joked and started up the engine while Donovan stood still, dead-faced in the moonlight. We weren't more than 10 feet apart, but it's the farthest away I've ever felt from someone.

When the noise of the golf cart was distant enough, I crawled out of the ditch beneath the porch and dusted myself off. I entered the cabin and found tables covered in red cloth, and banners hanging up on the walls, painted with golden crowns. On the center table, there were candles burning around a large black box tied with a single white string. I slid the string off of the box without disturbing the knot and, as I suspected, found a red leather binder inside.

On its cover were the golden stencils Daniel Friedman had described to me. THE BOOK in bold letters and a golden crown. It was directly in front of me.

I read it as quickly as someone can read a thing that's ruined his life, which I guess is to say, I didn't read it very quickly at all. With each page I felt another sting. It was describing the last year of my life. As if my whole life had been planned out to this point. And oh yes—

I found out what the Grunt is.

When I first read it, I couldn't believe how simple it was. When I read it again, I got so mad that I tore out half the page and threw it on the floor. Then I picked up the crumbled paper and read it again. Now I think I'll spit on it and stick it here in this journal:

...k for you.

The Grunt should be the person in your class who is not ugly or good-looking. Stupid or Smart. Mean or Nice. Funny or Boring. He should be the one person in your group most defined by what he is not.

Because, of course, the point of creating a Grunt is to demonstrate your own power over the way things are. The only obvious reason for him being the Grunt should be that you picked him. The Grunt is someone who does not know who he is. And you are someone who tells him who he is. He is the Grunt.

I have a feeling they'll be back soon, but I don't know what to do with this book. I can't just leave it, that's for sure. I can't let them do this to another kid next year, but if I steal it or destroy it, The Evil Three will know. What if they have a backup copy? They'd just replace it.

The Grunt is the person in your class who is most defined by what he is not. Someone who does not know who he is.

The more I read this, the truer it seems. You may not be a good principal, Tony Clark, but you're not dumb.

I look at Richard and Daniel and Clarence. Who are these kids?

They're Grunts and that's all. They've wholly absorbed that identity; their lives revolve around it. Richard became an angry maniac, Daniel a solitary weirdo, and Clarence an obsessive-compulsive. What were they before 6th grade? What carried over from their pre-Grunt lives?

The Evil Three have been gone for some time now. And I've been alone with my thoughts.

I've always seen myself as exceedingly normal. I prided myself on it, nothing weird about me at all. I've been a blank canvas for the Bully Bookers to paint their Grunt on.

I can't imagine this happening to someone like Jason Crazypants or even Colin Greene. They would have fought back, or ignored it and gone on living.

I was obsessed with *why* I was the Grunt. What made me the Grunt? But I totally accepted that I was the Grunt.

I never once said, This is not who I am. Because, maybe, I didn't know who I was, so I just let someone else tell me.

I never talked about it, not to Dad or Mom or Whitner, because I was ashamed.

Ashamed of the person they told me I was.

The Bully Book doesn't work if the Grunt has friends. It says it right here, **isolate the Grunt**. I see what they did with Melody and me. They were clever.

I have my yearbook here with me still. I opened it up to the page that Melody signed, and read what she wrote:

Dear Eric,

I am so sorry for what happened this year. At first it seemed like we were both embarrassed and avoiding each other. And then I kinda got over it, but thought you still didn't want to talk. Then the thing with Jason happened, and that's, like, a whole other story, but I still thought about you and was trying to make things better for you any way that I could.

I know that it didn't work out the way that I planned. I should have stopped going out with him when I realized that—I don't really know what I was thinking.

I just want to say that I'm sorry and I feel terrible, but you're still one of the best friends I've ever had.

I really hope I didn't screw it up completely and that we can be back to how we were someday.

Have a really good summer, Eric. Call me if you want to hang out.

—Melody

I see what I did wrong.

I played by the rules of The Book.

The Book told them to isolate me, and I helped it along. I didn't try and explain things to Melody. I didn't respond when she tried to talk to me. I thought I couldn't be her friend anymore, because she was wrapped up with the Bully Bookers and The Book.

Just how The Book wanted me to feel.

I should have been better to Colin. We could have gone through this year together, but I saw him as a tool, someone I needed to use to solve the mystery. I treated him like someone in my way, but he could have been a friend.

The Bully Book commanded and I obeyed. I followed every rule.

The Book changed me.

And now I'm going to change it. I've kept my journals with me all year, like a casebook. They're a record of my transformation into the Grunt. All my pain and struggles are in these pages—and now they'll be in The Bully Book, too.

I'm adding my journals to The Book, starting from the beginning. I'll blend them with the pages of The Bully Book itself, so they can't be easily unlinked. This is the other half of the story. The Grunt speaks.

The Evil Three won't read The Book before they pass it on. The first people to read this blend will be next year's Bully Bookers. I don't know how they'll react to it. I don't know what they'll do with it.

Future Bully Bookers: I'm talking to you.

I don't know if my story will speak to you.

If you have any heart at all, you'll stop. If you have any brains at all, you know I WILL STOP YOU.

If you've read this blended Bully Book, you'll know what I'm capable of. I've solved the mystery. I know your plans. And I will do everything in my power to make sure there is never again another Grunt.

Right now, I feel a kind of happiness. Not a carefree kind. I don't know if I'll ever feel that again. But I have the kind of gladness that comes with knowing exactly what you have to do.

I'm going back to my friends. I'll make up with Melody and I'll bring Colin into our circle.

I'm taking back my life. No one's dictating to me anymore.

And I'm exposing the madness.

If you are holding this book in your hands, I have a message for you:

The Grunt knows your secrets. He can't be contained. He has everything to gain . . . and you can only lose.

The Bully Book
By Tony Clark & Eric Haskins

Eric's Acknowledgments

My greatest thanks to Nick and Matt Lang for teaching me how to do this.

Hanna Pylväinen was my first reader, and she read the entire novel when I was only supposed to submit a short story in her writing class. But she still won't let me read her book!

Jennifer Allison gave me a chance and sent me to my excellent agent, Erica Rand Silverman. Erin Fitzsimmons designed this book beautifully. And my editor, Phoebe Yeh, has made this book better in immeasurable ways.

I'm forever indebted to all the good people at Team StarKid (who are really just my friends) for their incredible support and love. I don't know where I'd be without you.

Mom, Dad, and Alyssa: I love you all like family, so I'm glad it worked out that way.

About the Author

The Bully Book is loosely based on events that happened to Eric Kahn Gale in elementary school. When he was eleven years old, he felt like the whole class was conspiring against him. Everyone used the same insults and nicknames, and there didn't seem to be a safe corner of the room or moment in the day.

Looking back on this now, it probably wasn't the organized, well-run machine he thought it was—but in a tough spot like that, perspective is hard to come by. This is why he was inspired to write *The Bully Book*, his first book.

Eric really wants to know what you think about *The Bully Book*. Please write to him at thebullybook@gmail.com.

Resources

Here are some websites and help lines for those seeking information.

BullyBust:

www.schoolclimate.org/bullybust

National Education Association:

www.nea.org/home/NEABullyFreeSchools.html

The Bully Project:

http://thebullyproject.startempathy.org

Stop Bullying:

www.stopbullying.gov

National Bullying Prevention Center:

www.pacer.org/bullying

The Bully Book
Copyright © 2011, 2013 by Eric Kahn Gale
All rights reserved. Printed in the United States of America. No part of this book may be used or reproduced in any manner whatsoever without written permission except in the case of brief quotations embodied in critical articles and reviews.
For information address HarperCollins Children's Books, a division of HarperCollins Publishers, 10 East 53rd Street, New York, NY 10022.
www.harpercollinschildrens.com

Library of Congress Cataloging-in-Publication Data
Gale, Eric Kahn, 1986–
The Bully Book / by Eric Kahn Gale. — First edition.
pages cm
"Originally published in a different format as an ebook by the author"—Copyright page.
Loosely based on events from the author's life.
Summary: In this story told alternately through journal entries and instructions from a bullying manual, sixth-grader Eric embarks on a quest to find the reason why he is being teased and tormented in middle school.
ISBN 978-0-06-212513-2 (pbk.)
[1. Bullying—Fiction. 2. Middle schools—Fiction. 3. Schools—Fiction. 4. Diaries—Fiction.] I. Title.
PZ7.G13134Bu 2012 2012050677
[Fic]—dc23 CIP
AC

Typography by Erin Fitzsimmons
13 14 15 16 17 LP/RRDH 10 9 8 7 6 5 4 3 2 1
❖
First paperback edition, 2013
Originally published in a different format as an ebook by the author.

Q&A with author Eric Kahn Gale

Q&A with author Eric Kahn Gale

What is the typical day in the life of Eric Kahn Gale? Tell us about it.
I wake up and am greeted by a dog named Bowser, who very badly has to go to the bathroom. Dogs aren't technically allowed in my apartment building, so I tell him to be very quiet and we sneak down five flights of a back stairway to the parking garage. We dodge the apartment security people and make our way to a park. Then we sneak back up and do this over again about five times throughout the day.

In between all that, I try to get some writing done.

What is your favorite color?
Green, because it reminds me of plants.

What are your top five favorite movies?

1. Disney's *The Hunchback of Notre Dame*. I guess there's a part of me that still feels like an outcast, and I just love it when Quasimodo finds acceptance at the end of the movie.
2. *The Lion King*. It's so epic, beautiful, and funny. Sometimes I go through periods where I just watch the movie and the behind-the-scenes features on the DVD over and over.
3. The Lord of the Rings trilogy. I've seen all three movies multiple times (the extended editions, mind you), but have spent many more hours watching the extra features. Sometimes I buy DVDs of movies that I love just for the extra features and never get around to watching the actual movie. *The Hunchback of Notre Dame* has the skimpiest extra features of any Disney DVD, and it makes me boil.

4. *Pocahontas*. This movie definitely has some flaws, but if you watch it for sequences and songs, it's some of the best stuff Disney has ever done.
5. *The Incredibles*. On a pure storytelling level, this is one of the most fun movies you could ever watch.

What are your top five favorite foods?

1. Pad See Ew is probably my favorite thing to get at a restaurant. It's this tasty Thai dish made with rice noodles and broccoli.
2. Cheez-It® crackers are high on my favorite foods list. I'm pretty much keeping them out of #1 from embarrassment.
3. There was this veggie burger I had once that was made out of mushrooms and all these vegetables, and oh man, it was so good. I've been looking to have that burger again for a while.
4. Oyster mushrooms. Man, these things are so delicious when stir-fried with some eggs. I've been trying to grow them in my house on old ground coffee beans (long story).
5. Cheez-It® Reduced Fat crackers. Because I gotta watch my health.

What is your favorite kind of music? Your favorite band or musical artist? What do you love about him/her/them?

I really like this band called the Decemberists. A lot of their songs are from the point of view of a particular character, often from a specific time and place in history. I just love music lyrics with strong stories.

What is your favorite book of all time? Your favorite books as a kid?

I don't really have a favorite book, but the only two books that

I've read more than three times each are J.D. Salinger's *Nine Stories* and Elizabeth Gilbert's *Eat, Pray, Love. Nine Stories* is kind of what it sounds like: nine short stories about different people. The stories have a texture and feel that I love. It was the first collection of short stories that I ever read, and that on top of it just being an amazing little book, I found myself reading it again and again. *Eat, Pray, Love* is about a woman who feels lost in life. I can definitely relate to that feeling. I first read the book after I graduated from college, moved away from home, and was having an especially hard time. The woman in the book gets into meditation and writes about how much it helps her. Meditation is kind of like pushups for your mind—you focus on one specific thought and try to empty your brain of everything else. I started meditating around the time I read the book and found it did wonders for me too.

As a kid, I was also a big fan of short mystery books. I loved Encyclopedia Brown, You Be the Jury, and the Clue series. I always wanted to figure out the solution to the mystery. If the book was written really well, the ending always blew my mind, and on the rare occasion that I figured it out, I felt really smart. But sometimes it was impossible to guess the solution and that drove me nuts.

I tried to make the mystery in *The Bully Book* something readers could solve.

Do you have a favorite author? Or a few favorite authors? If so, who and why?

My favorite author is this guy named David Foster Wallace even though I've never read any of his fiction. This might make people reading this poke fun at me, because he's very famous for his fiction writing. But I've read nearly all of his essays.

He writes nonfiction that is incredibly interesting and full of fascinating observations, and I just love getting to share his intense view of the world.

What are your ten writing tips for any readers who are also aspiring authors?

1. Find some friends that like writing too. Developing ideas with my talented friends has been my bedrock as a writer.
2. Write down notes to yourself whenever you have an idea for a story.
3. Just sit in front of your computer and type what you're thinking; that can get your writing-mind going.
4. Read books that are directed at aspiring screenplay writers. Screenplays have a more rigid and well-defined form than novels, and while some people criticize movies for being "formulaic," that formula is the product of writers working over the years to perfect effective kinds of storytelling. I find they will teach you more about basic story theory than books about novel writing, or any writing.
5. Read books and watch movies to soak up the way the story is transmitted to you. What shape does the story take?
6. Write out a Beat Sheet, or outline, of the major points in the plot and the "beats" or sections of the story.
7. Figure out the structure of your book early in the process. Deciding on the alternating nature of *The Bully Book* really dictated almost everything I did from that point forward.
8. Don't worry about getting scenes (or characters) perfect the first time. Sketch out the story again and again in multiple drafts. I

rewrote *The Bully Book* seven times.

9. Figure out if writing to a certain type of music or sound helps you. I have a good friend who writes to white noise; I prefer to make a Pandora station and then listen to that every time I'm writing a book. For *The Bully Book* I listened to the same twenty or so songs over and over for about two and a half years.
10. Don't be lazy. Serve the story as best as you can. Challenge yourself to write something good.

Have you had a role model in your career as a writer? Who inspires you to be the best writer you can be?

My friends Nick and Matt Lang are the best writers I know. They are very critical and very talented. I am almost always thinking about trying to impress them when I write.

How did you get the idea for *The Bully Book*?

I heard a story on "This American Life" (on NPR) where a first grader told an interviewer that he saw his bully with a book that taught you how to be mean to people. The interviewer thought that was weird, so he asked the teacher and librarian if the kids had such a book.

Of course, that would never be allowed in school, they answered. No one would ever publish a book like that. The interviewer concluded that the little first grader was so scared of his bully that he imagined seeing the book. Wasn't that sad?

It wouldn't be a published book, I thought, it would be something that the kids wrote and passed around themselves. THE BULLY BOOK. What an idea! I had been walking around listening to the show on my headphones, but I ripped them off immediately and ran into a Starbucks. I sat down and wrote out the first paragraph of *The Bully Book* on my iPhone.

Did your personal experiences shape *The Bully Book* at all?

When I was in elementary school I was pretty terribly bullied. I was called all sorts of names, and it felt like my every move was mocked. My fifth grade teacher took every Monday off for two months to visit her sick father. On Mondays we went around the class, each kid saying one of the week's vocabulary words. On the first week my teacher was out, one of my tormentors had the word "yonder." He used it in a sentence. "I can see Eric Gale's big head over yonder field." Everyone laughed and the substitute teacher did nothing about it. Soon everyone in the class was using their vocab words to make fun of me and it went on like this for months.

It felt like there was some conspiracy amongst the class to make me miserable. I realize now that wasn't true, but it's how I felt at the time.

My family moved districts between fifth and sixth grades, and in my new school I was a normal kid. The difference always struck me as strange. If there was something wrong with me it would have traveled to the new school, and I would have been bullied there. But it was as though someone just needed to be the lowest at my old school, and for some reason they choose me.

The format of *The Bully Book* is unique, because it alternates between the point of view of the bully and the bully's victim. How did you come up with this?

Once I knew there would be an actual "Bully Book" in the novel and that the main character would be searching for it, I knew that the audience would be dying to read it, too. So peppering it into the main narrative of the book came naturally.

Did any of your characters take on the attributes of people you knew in real life? Which character was your favorite to write?
My favorite character was Eric, because he's really just an eleven-year-old me. Colin was enjoyable too because he's based on a real kid I knew (who was also named Colin, oops!) and was this kind of gross guy who was my only friend.

Have kids reached out to you to share their bullying experiences?
Yes, absolutely. Whenever I receive positive mail from readers, it delights me, but especially when the readers themselves have had problems with bullying and write me that the book has helped them in some way. I hope the reading experience can give them strength and the courage to share their story.

Because through all my searching, I believe that kids can only save themselves from bullying by knowing strongly who they are and what they love and allowing no one else to tell them otherwise.

With regard to bullying in schools today, how can readers help make a difference?
I think the number one thing readers can do is talk to the kids in their lives. I still don't know why children gang up on each other, and I don't know how to stop it. Parents should absolutely be asking their kids as often as possible what their lives are like in school, and teachers should make it clear that bullying won't be tolerated. But the real interactions that take place between children aren't governed by adults, and the only real solution is inner strength.

ASSOCIATED HEBREW SCHOOLS
252 FINCH AVE. W.
TORONTO, ONTARIO
M2R 1M9